TREACHERY IN THE YARD

TREACHERY IN THE YARD

A NIGERIAN THRILLER

ADIMCHINMA IBE

MINOTAUR BOOKS

THOMAS DUNNE BOOKS

NEW YORK

This is a work of fiction. All of the characters, organizations, and events portrayed in this novel are either products of the author's imagination or are used fictitiously.

A THOMAS DUNNE BOOK FOR MINOTAUR BOOKS.
An imprint of St. Martin's Publishing Group.

www.thomasdunnebooks.com
www.minotaurbooks.com

Edited by Victor Schwartzman

Library of Congress Cataloging-in-Publication Data

Ibe, Adimchinma, 1977–
    Treachery in the yard : a Nigerian thriller / Adimchinma Ibe. — 1st ed.
        p. cm.
    ISBN 978-0-312-58593-8
    1. Police—Nigeria—Fiction.   2. Nigeria—Fiction.   I. Title.
    PR9387.9.I125T74 2010
    823'.92—dc22

                                                                2009046153

First Edition: August 2010

10   9   8   7   6   5   4   3   2   1

To the memory of my late father

ACKNOWLEDGMENTS

I couldn't have made it this far without the help and support of so many people and friends. Obviously, my family are without a doubt the biggest and most influential supporters of mine, but there are also others who have to be mentioned who have had a big impact on my life. I'd like to thank:

Victor Schwartzman, who became an acquaintance of mine in 2005. It has been, and still is, such an amazing thrill for me to have the writer from Winnipeg edit my manuscripts purely on a voluntary basis. Thanks, mate, for all the editing, advice, and help whenever I needed it. It's been great having you to guide me and support me on this incredible journey.

My most cherished Sister Lavender Ugwa, who has been incredible with the support she has given me over the years. Dearest, you deserve a lot of the credit. Thanks for your help in getting me to this level.

My mother, Patricia Ibe, who believed in me when no one else did. When I started, you were the only one who told me I could do it. It is not a surprise to you that I did it. And my brothers, Fortune and Chinedu, for their words of encouragement along the way.

Marcia Markland, without you I wouldn't have had the opportunity to be published. Diana Szu, and now Kat Brzozowski, for supporting me throughout this entire process. And everyone at Thomas Dunne Books/St. Martin's Press for your support.

CHAPTER ONE

The lead officer briefed us as we walked through the chaotic scene. Burnt pieces of furniture, blackened soot, and plaster were everywhere. Smoke billowed from the dying flames. Some medics carried the wounded and dead from the inferno while others searched for survivors.

Police from every district had been called to the scene. They were having a hard time controlling the surging crowd. They all wanted to see. The heat from the fire, combined with the heat from the sun, made the scene feel like hell itself.

The explosion destroyed Pius Okpara's garage and most of his home. Okpara was running for the statehouse. He was an important politician in the middle of an angry nomination battle to head the National Conservative Party's banner. He had initially been his party's only candidate, but then Dr. Vincent Puene came into the race, and suddenly Okpara had to deal with an opponent.

Now Okpara would have to win the party primaries. If he survived.

Okpara lived in GRA Phase II—the Government Reservation Area, densely populated with some of Port Harcourt's wealthiest.

Okpara's compound was large and spacious. The main building was at the far side of the only entrance into the compound. A high fence and an equally massive bulletproof iron gate painted brown protected the area. The building itself was a modern design duplex with wall-to-wall cream Italian marble. Aluminum long-span roofing sheets and wire gauze lined the top of the fencing. There was a basketball court that I bet was rarely used unless his son visited Nigeria, which rarely happened.

Here and there in the destruction were pieces of artwork, objects of aesthetic beauty and chinaware of high value. He must have a strong appreciation for the finer things in life. Only one thing was missing: a swimming pool. Perhaps he was not a good swimmer.

The bomb had been placed in the garage, and when it went off, it took with it the garage's large front door, the rooms above, and the walls. What was left of the garage was black soot and iron rods. Whoever placed the bomb took their work seriously. And the house? What was left was in flames, with firefighters from the Divisional Fire Service hosing it down. Two house staff members had been found dead already, and three who were seriously injured were on their way to the hospital. Okpara himself had apparently not been seriously injured, but of course, he was the first one rushed off in an ambulance, given his status. Mrs. Okpara had not been at home, in fact she was not even in the country. She was visiting their son, who was a police officer in England.

The neighboring buildings were not too badly damaged. The worst damage was to the home to the right of Okpara's duplex, a house owned by a retired military officer, Major Augustine Eke.

The two buildings were separated by a twelve-foot-high concrete fence. Augustine had been at the military officers' golf course and had come home five minutes after the explosion. He was lucky to have been away; his wall facing Okpara's house was riddled with shrapnel, the windows of his house blown out.

On the other side of Okpara's house was a duplex, which was set back on the far side of the garage area, so the damage was not as bad. Six windows were broken, the shattered glass crunching under us as my partner, Olufemi Adegbola—Femi for short— and I walked through the wreckage. It was noisy, dirty, and smoky, with the smell of dirty politics in the air.

After talking with the lead officer, I had him assign some police to canvass the area for witnesses. There were not too many police—most were busy organizing the crime scene and ensuring everyone had been evacuated from the damaged or destroyed homes. We all felt the bombing had been a professional job; the device had been well placed in the garage, which could not have been easy given Okpara's security.

Emergency crews were looking for other bombs, live electrical wires, anything that could be a danger. They were fine at their jobs. For Femi and myself, all we needed for the moment was an overview of what had happened, and to stand back and let the field staff do their work.

I watched Darlington Nnadozie, the officer leading the bomb squad, set up his equipment. He was a young officer in his prime. His lean frame made him look like an athlete rather than a police officer. We knew each other, though our work did not often bring us together.

Darlington was a warm, enthusiastic individual, typically very bright and full of potential. But he had one problem: He placed no importance on details in an investigation. I can become obsessed with minor details. These details may seem to be extremely unimportant, but in reality, they can be critical. But what could I expect from a detective who only has computers and electronic gadgets to play with? He was a forensics man. He had no real contact with people.

Mostly I dealt with people who were shot, stabbed, or poisoned. Rarely were my homicides the result of an explosion. The average homicidal Nigerian could not afford to bomb anyone, and blowing someone up is very expensive and requires planning. Most murders are impulsive and done on the cheap, with whatever is at hand: a knife, a hammer, a fist. Bombs usually mean organization and advance planning and money.

I walked over as he struggled into his coveralls to start his job.

"Hello, Darlington," I said. "Nice morning to be outside, eh?" We shook hands. "What do we have here?"

He shrugged. "Five to six more hours of hard work. Can't tell you anything worthwhile yet. Maybe you'll want to go and interview some witnesses, or drink some beer, or whatever it is you do."

"Beer? Fine with me. Though Captain Akpan might not approve."

"He would if you were field staff."

"I'd rather be in my office than crawl through the rubble. I'm happier interviewing witnesses. Even when they lie a lot."

He shrugged again. "Will you bring back a beer, at least?"

"What makes you think I'm coming back?"

He and his crew went to work. The lead officer came up to tell me his men had turned up some witnesses. One of his staff led me to the home across the street, where I met Mrs. Naomi Karibi. She was the wife of a state judge, and the mother of two teenage boys and a daughter. She had been the only one home, and described seeing a heavy-set man, over six feet tall, driving an old weather-beaten white Peugeot 305 away from the area after the explosion. She had seen the car a few times in the neighborhood the last few days. She deliberately stayed aware of anyone or anything suspicious in the neighborhood—her judge husband had made his fair share of enemies.

She said that she had seen the man walking into the compound before the explosion. How long before, she was not sure. She had been relaxing on her patio. She saw him park and walk into the compound. She had gotten a cell phone call, and was talking to her daughter when the garage blew apart. The man ran from the scene to his car, holding a white kerchief to his face. He was bleeding from the ear. She had time to get his license number and write it down. My kind of woman—well, she was a judge's wife.

"I didn't see which way he drove off, but he was the one who set the bomb. Why else would he have run away? I had thought he was a politician who had come to see Okpara, like the rest of them. People often come on a pilgrimage to Okpara. There was nothing strange about him, until after the explosion."

"What makes you think he set off the bomb? If he set it off, wouldn't he have first gotten away?"

"He ran out. He was bleeding. If he was legitimate, why was he running? I was just ready to leave the patio to see where he drove off when I heard the second explosion."

"Second explosion? There was a second?"

"Oh yes. Bigger than the first. That was when the garage caved in and caught fire."

Femi and I interviewed, separately, more witnesses. Other people also saw the man enter the Peugeot immediately after the explosions, his ear bleeding. The car had been parked near the Karibis' home.

Darlington's group had finished their initial examination of the blast scene and was in the process of collecting evidence by the time we were through interviewing witnesses. He thought the bomb was on a raised platform inches from the floor—otherwise the impact crater would have been larger—and that it may have detonated prematurely. He thought there was nothing tricky about the bomb, that it probably detonated on a table. However, a larger blast followed, in another part of the garage—that was the one that took the garage out, along with part of the adjoining house.

As I finished my talk with Darlington, I noticed Okpara's personal assistant, Stephen Wike, walking with Kola Badmus, a newspaper reporter I knew. Wike was wearing a long-sleeved buba, pants, and a Fila hat.

He looked nervous. Maybe he was upset that his boss had been nearly blown apart, maybe it was something else. Today, though, he seemed to have lost his ability to remain unruffled. I approached him.

"Who are you?" he asked sharply. "I have a general press conference in about thirty minutes. You can ask your questions then. I'm doing an exclusive here."

I brought out my badge. "Homicide. Detective Tamunoemi Peterside. I want to ask you about the bombing."

He backed off a bit. "You're police?"

Kola did not say anything, but he did not back away, either. He stayed, listening.

I put away the badge. "You were in the house?"

"Yes. It was terrifying. I'm lucky to be alive."

"Any ideas who was behind it?"

"No."

"Did Okpara receive any threatening calls or letters?"

"Not that I know of."

"Who hated him this much?"

"No one I know of. I don't think his opponents would try to kill him, at least not like this." Something about his tone was not right. He was afraid, of me. Why would he be worried about the police?

"What about Dr. Puene?"

"I can't see it. Yes, Puene is an opponent. But I can't imagine he'd try to murder anyone. That's absurd." However, he failed the eye-contact test.

This was getting interesting.

"I'd like to talk with you some more later," I told him. He just nodded and, with apparent relief, went back to answering Kola's questions as I walked away.

It would be hours before forensics came up with more than what we already knew. I decided to pay a visit to Dr. Puene, Okpara's opponent.

I phoned Staff Sergeant Okoro and asked him to run the license-plate number Mrs. Karibi gave us. "Femi and I are on our way to Dr. Puene's. Keep any information you get on that car until we get back. Only I should get it. Clear, sergeant?"

"Yes, sir."

"Good."

Okoro was older than even Chief and me. He had joined the force as a young school leaver thirty years ago, and was billed to retire soon. He rose through the ranks to become a staff sergeant. An experienced police officer but a dweeb. We all wondered what he did with his money. He did not buy clothes and had worn one pair of shoes for as long as I could remember. He had left his family in the village to live a better life, but he was not a bad man, just selfish. He was honest, friendly, and competent—at least when he was sober.

I sighed, then took out my cell and phoned Freda Agboke,

my girlfriend. I had to tell her I would miss lunch. The explosion and investigation were all the explanation she needed. We agreed to do dinner instead. Then I went back to my car with Femi, and we drove to Rumuokoro, to speak with Dr. Puene.

CHAPTER TWO

The estate in Rumuokoro had no paved streets, but the owners had started paving them on their own, without government help. They had the money to do it. They even had industrial generating sets for a private power supply—there were regular power failures throughout Port Harcourt. They sunk boreholes and built overhead water tanks for storage. They even arranged their own security. Rumuokoro was its own little world, filled with big people.

At Dr. Puene's, a uniformed guard stood in front of a big red-painted iron gate.

"Police," I told the guard. When he just stood there, I showed him my badge. He opened the gate.

The compound was big, with three buildings. Paradise on earth . . . for Port Harcourt, anyway. The buildings were big enough so each was a compound of its own. Painted a cream color, with dark red roofing, the buildings looked alike, differing only in size and shape. A gleaming black Toyota Limited SUV with tinted glass stood in the driveway. When I got out of the car I straightened my suit. Best to look nice for the rich. We got out and started for the front door of the largest building, not wasting any time with the supplicants milling about, waiting to see the doctor, hoping for some largesse.

A mobile policeman in a very crisp uniform and holding a combat rifle guarded the front door. He looked too well fed to be Nigerian police. Who said living in the court of the superrich doesn't have benefits? Not me.

I again pulled out my badge. "Police. Here to see Dr. Puene."

He saluted.

That amused me, but I said, "Thank you, sergeant." It is always good to be polite to people bigger than you are.

We followed him inside to the foyer, which looked even richer than outside. The furniture was all imported, the curtains were Italian silk, very expensive paintings hung on the walls—or at least, they looked expensive. They certainly were big and had plenty of colors.

The inside walls were done in a cream color. The furniture matched, in leather. There was a crafted leafless tree with several lighted bulbs, all imported, illuminating the foyer. The air-conditioning was wonderful.

If the foyer was exquisite, the living room was even more so. I walked through a large sculpted archway to enter the room. It was huge. Here, the furniture was all white leather with yellow lace covers. There was a wrought-iron center table, a cream marbled floor, a chocolate brown, wooden-paned ceiling fan with gold trimmings. The red wool curtains were Italian. More expensive paintings.

Strangest, there was a fireplace. That was a good laugh. A fireplace in the tropics? Were these folks expecting it to snow in

Port Harcourt? Some people can't give up their borrowed cultures.

That led me to wondering about Mrs. Puene, who was originally from California. Rumor had it that she had returned to America after just three weeks of slugging it out here in the tropical heat. She had come down with sunstroke and had rushed back to a cooler climate. She had married the young Nigerian doctor, who was studying at a university in the States, and, as their wedding gift, her father had solely financed Puene's private practice in Los Angeles. After a long time there, they left their sixteen-year-old son and fourteen-year-old daughter back in the States and moved to Nigeria this past April. Bad time to be in Africa for Mrs. Puene, a first-timer. The heat peaks at that time of the year. No one blamed the white woman. She never thought that marrying an African would mean having to actually live in Africa.

We came to a large room. The sergeant entered in front of us, announced us, and then we stood in the presence of the man himself.

Dr. Puene had a high forehead and a receding chin, a bad combination. He was about six feet tall and oozed power. He had keen brown eyes and thick black hair. Clean shaven and robust, he struck me as a natural-born leader, at least in his well-tailored American suit. He would have made the late Afro juju maestro from Nigeria cry. The way he carried himself spoke of a man who had surmounted all sorts of challenges, a man in charge. A medical doctor, successful by all standards. And an America-trained gynecologist.

He had started his campaign shortly after returning to Nigeria. He said the least he could do was listen to his people, opening a new era for the Ogoni in the politics of Rivers State. The Ogonis' history was an ongoing struggle against the degradation of their lands as a result of oil drilling, the suffering of their people, governmental neglect, lack of social services, and the political marginalization they endured in Nigeria. But he struck me as the type who was probably not as interested in opening up opportunities for his people as he was driven to get power. To me, he seemed the type of man who was prepared to succeed at any cost, including bombing his opponent. He also was no fool, and not a man given to errors. If he had planned the bombing, he would have ensured it would not be traced back to him.

"Good morning, Doctor," I said, walking up to him. "Sorry to bother you. I'm Homicide Detective Peterside and this is Detective Olufemi Adegbola. State police."

He smiled and shook our hands as if he meant it. "Very good, then. What can I do for you, officers? I don't have too much time, you saw the people waiting outside."

"It shouldn't be long. We have some questions."

"You said you are Homicide? Why do you want to talk to me? Who's your Oga?"

We call our superior officers *Oga* as a mark of respect. "I'm sure you know."

"Yes. I do." His face was hard to read—he would smile whether he liked or hated you. "I have achieved a certain station in life, detective. If Homicide wants to speak to me for some reason, I'll talk to your Oga."

I ignored the barely veiled threat. "Okpara's house has been bombed."

"I've been phoned."

"Do you know anything about it?"

"Of course not. The call was the first I'd heard."

"You're running against Okpara to be the candidate for governorship for your party."

"So?"

"You have a motive. We have to follow up on all possibilities."

He shook his head, dismissive. "This is a waste of my time. We are political rivals, not gangsters." He walked away, taking out a cell phone. "This conversation is over."

Puene, like many politicians in Nigeria, had difficulty seeing things from outside his own perspective. He had little patience with people who did not see things his way. He showed himself to be a forceful, intimidating, and overbearing individual. This had the potential to be a real problem for the yankee-trained doctor-turned-politician, as it could cost him allies.

Well, maybe interviewing him was a stupid wild guess, but it felt good to needle the jerk. We walked out, Femi trying to be invisible. The primaries were twelve days away. Violence was always in the air to begin with, and this race was close.

It was a long drive back to headquarters. We took Ikwerre Road to Diobu. By Nigerian standards, the roads were smooth. By any other standards, as Bette Davis had said, you had to be prepared for a bumpy ride. Large potholes loomed everywhere and were hard to avoid, the asphalt washed away by erosion to expose red earth.

There were scattered stalls along the roads. People chatted in the roadside markets. Drivers honked impatiently while noise from the many repair shops was deafening; it sounded like a thousand voices were shouting and cursing all at once. The carbon monoxide pumped into the atmosphere from the car and truck exhaust pipes made it difficult to breathe. The public housing was situated close to the roads, with garbage littering the streets. When the rain came, it got very flooded, making it difficult for cars to pass and a living hell for pedestrians.

I sighed. Port Harcourt is not all about filth and dirt and

disarray, but it certainly seemed like it much of the time. Most people lived in stench, say along Creek Road, the center of Port Harcourt. It was much nicer to live in neighborhoods that had playgrounds, where the noise level was low, the taps flowed with water, and working streetlights were taken for granted.

But that was in the Government Reservation Area. Elsewhere, tap water was unreliable, forcing many people to rely on water tankers and *Mai-ruwa* (water hawkers). Power outages were almost routine in the rest of Port Harcourt, where you could at times go for days without electricity. Too bad for those who did not live in the Government Reservation Areas.

CHAPTER THREE

We soon arrived at headquarters, and I was able to stop philoso-phizing, and return to work.

When Femi and I walked in, a news story on the Okpara bombing was on the TV in the common room. Mrs. Karibi, the judge's wife, was interviewed about what she had seen. That was too bad—I did not like my witnesses exposed.

It was past six in the evening when I called it a day.

"I'm off," I told Femi. "Get on with the report. I'll review it when you're finished."

"I'll have it ready tomorrow morning."

"And Femi . . ."

"Yes?"

"We'll have to keep an eye on Wike, Okpara's assistant. He didn't act normal. Maybe it was the bombing that had him jumpy, but it felt like something else. He knew more than he let on."

"Sure, boss. Whatever you say."

With that I drove off. By now it was 6:20. I went home to change into something more relaxed, then drove to Freda's.

Her place was far enough from the refinery fires that kept part of Port Harcourt unnaturally lit so that it was dark by the time I got to her place, dark enough so if you looked up, you could see stars. I rarely looked up at the stars—what was the point? Freda's apartment was a three-bedroom modern bungalow, part of a building complex wired to a giant industrial generator that supplied private power in case of outages. Her complex also provided clean water, pumping it into a massive overhead tank. The rent was high, high enough to keep civil servants, police detectives, and other ordinary people outside, looking in—just as we might look up at the stars we could never reach. But Freda could afford it. Her job paid very well. She could afford leather seats in her living room; mine were done in fabric. The seats were more like a very long cream-colored couch, placed in an L shape.

I never understood her dislike for paintings. Nothing hung on the walls except for a clock. Rubber-tiled flooring matched the color of the walls.

Where she had really gone overboard was her array of electronics. A twenty-one-inch flat-screen TV, the latest on the market, accompanied by an LG mini–theater system. Her bedroom was a lush ash with a white carpet, with an Arabian rug beside the mahogany bed. By her bedside, on a small night table, was a portrait of Christ with the crown of thorns.

Her kitchen showed the most effort. It made my own kitchen look like the cheaply furnished room it was. She had a standing gas cooker with an oven for baking, a superdeluxe Zanussi fridge, and a multifunction food processor that looked ready for space travel.

She opened the door, wearing the dress I had first seen her in. "This is for our anniversary," she said, smiling.

I swallowed. I'd thought our anniversary was next week.

"Like it?" she asked.

"Of course. I remember that night. I cherish it. Just as I cherish you."

Without any gift, I then avoided saying anything else by kissing her. I did not fool her for a second. She laughed as soon as our lips parted. I think I had enough smarts to look embarrassed. We went down the stairs to where my car was parked. I did not like it that she was always a step ahead of me. And she always was.

"I'm taking you somewhere exotic for the night. You'll love it." Where, I didn't know yet, of course.

"Oh?"

"Somewhere cozy," I said as we got into the car.

"Where, exactly?" She was on to me, but we both knew that.

"If I tell you, it won't be a surprise."

I thought quickly as I drove, trying to look as if I knew where I was going—I was probably going straight to the hell reserved for inattentive boyfriends. I thought about the dress she had put on and, in a flash of semi-brilliance, took her to the place we'd gone for our first date—Protea Hotel.

I kept us going with sweet talk until we pulled up outside. When she saw where we were, her lips gave me a gift. "This is the most romantic thing you have done in a long time," she said. She appeared happy; that was all that counted. I would accept being shallow right now.

We went inside. It was exquisite as ever and expensive, but I didn't mind the hole it bored in my wallet; it was better than Freda boring a hole in my head.

It cost quite a few naira, definitely on the pricey end for

continental food. If we had tried other places we could have had the same food for less, but that was not nearly as romantic. This was the scene of our first date.

After dinner I took her home, stopping the car in front of her apartment, engine still running, headlights still on.

She looked at me, seeing the message.

Should I go in? I had not remembered our anniversary: what did that say? "I have to go back to work I brought home from the office. I talked about today over dinner. You know. Politicians blowing each other up. The pressure's on and Chief wants his report."

She knew I was lying. I could tell she was hurt, but she just gave me a kiss and left me there. Maybe she'd known all along. Maybe she had her own doubts about the relationship. Maybe she knew how much rope to give me.

I drove on, wondering why I was such a son of a bitch. My cell phone rang. It was Femi.

"Night duty received a call from the Karibis. Remember them?"

I didn't like what I heard in his voice. "Sure. The witness."

"Five minutes ago, some people tried to break into their home."

"I'll see you there."

I was at the Karibis' twenty minutes later. Across the street, the bombing scene was dark and bleak. Femi and other police officers met me as I drove up and parked.

"What happened?" I asked Femi as I got out of my car.

"Someone tried to break in through the back door. His dog barking woke up Judge Karibi. He and his wife were in an upstairs bedroom. He looked through the window and saw a light flash in the backyard."

"And?"

"He called out, thinking it was his night watchman. It wasn't. The torchlight was turned off right away, and he saw two men run from the compound and spring over the wall but he saw neither clearly enough to provide a good description."

The Karibis were sitting in the back of a patrol car. They felt safer there. I approached them.

"My colleague told me some people tried to break into your house."

I heard the story straight from Karibi. When he had tried to call the police, the line was dead. He ended up using his cell to call us. The backyard light was off, and I saw a moment later that it and all the other outside bulbs had been broken.

If the assailant was merely a thief, it would be one of those coincidences that only happen in poorly written novels. Of all the witnesses we had spoken to earlier, only Mrs. Karibi had been on TV. None of the other homes had been broken into, and the Karibis' car remained untouched, parked just outside the fence, an easy touch.

The lead officer left some policemen to guard the Karibis' home and patrol officers to comb the neighborhood with instructions to arrest and detain any stragglers until we verified their identities and what they were doing in the area.

It was time to go.

I drove to my apartment. It had two bedrooms, which was good, although I did not really need the second one. It was the best I could afford on my salary of N18,000 per month (without bribes).

The whole neighborhood was dark.

The power had gone out again. Most outages lasted around two hours. Old transformers breaking down cause some power outages; those outages can take a day or two to correct.

Power outages are more than sitting in the dark. The refrigerator stops running and everything starts to thaw and get warm. Not good if you live in a tropical climate. The air becomes stuffy and extremely hot.

It had been a stinker of a day.

CHAPTER FOUR

I woke the next morning, got out of bed and into my routine: wash, dress, put on my holster and slip in my piece, put my badge in my pocket, grab the car keys from the side table, finally let myself out of the apartment. But I grumbled all the way through. I was running late because my alarm clock had not turned on: the power was still off. This was common. Often you had to pay a bribe to get electricity initially turned on for your home. When the electricity was on, it was expensive and unreliable.

When I left, as always I wedged a piece of paper in the door frame. If, when I returned, the paper was no longer crammed in the door frame, but lying on the floor, I knew my apartment had an unexpected visitor. The paper was my little borrowing from an old James Bond movie, *Dr. No*. Bond used a strand of hair, I use paper. Simple, but effective—and necessary. You never know who might visit you when you are not there. To survive, you must be one step ahead.

I stepped outside. The morning was fresh and warm. It would get hot before long, and then you would sweat under the sun, but for now, I savored the morning's freshness as I breathed the warm air.

I walked over to my car and got into it, pushing the water bottles off the driver's seat—in this heat, it was a good idea to always have a drink ready, and I kept a supply of water always available. I backed out and made some good progress until I ran into a holdup coming close to the Flyover at the Isaac Boro Park.

I called Femi to tell him I would be late and he told me Chief wanted to see me as soon as I got there. Traffic began to move again so I eased off the gear, let in the clutch, and continued on my way to work.

As I approached police headquarters, it looked anything but imposing in the morning sunlight. Once it was indeed magnificent, but that was fifty years ago, at the height of the Colonial Police Force—long, long before the oil money arrived to create a dark polluted slick over Nigeria. Back then, the buildings were new, alive with power, their brick walls the color of dried blood (a color borrowed from some of the prisoners held inside). Since those golden days, the heat, the damp, and the lack of care had relentlessly scrubbed the magnificence away, leaving only a shabby exterior. The former glory, like Ozymandias, the once King of Kings, was a very distant memory.

Over the years, new offices were added to the original building in the large courtyard, new buildings gradually added to the old, and finally a separate new building was constructed nearby. Naturally, senior police officials grabbed the top floors of the new building, treating themselves far better than the Colonial Police had, as befitted their greater power. The new building was a one-minute walk from the original building, painted white, looking new, but the distance between the two was longer, deeper, and wider than the open sewers that ran through the Diobu Zone.

It was no coincidence that the first major construction project started by the military junta when it came to power in the eighties was the State Police Building. Maintaining power, keeping control—it was as vital to Nigeria as keeping the oil wells pumping. The State Police had made certain their offices were housed in the largest building in the complex, towering over the old Colonial Police Force building—the new power overshadowing the old. The top floor offices were palatial in comparison to the original offices: more spacious, fitted with air conditioners, modern furniture, and plants. They even had secretaries. In sharp contrast was my stuffy ten-by-eight-foot space, located just across the Yard. My office was barely large enough to contain two old desks, five chairs (three of which you could sit in without any appreciable risk), and a filing cabinet longing for retirement. At least I had room enough to stretch my legs, which was more than what most of my colleagues had.

The lower cadre police officials who did the actual work were still housed in the old offices. Myself, for example: Detective Tamunoemi Peterside, Lieutenant, Homicide.

Homicide was busy. Although unemployment was a major issue in Nigeria, I did not have to worry about my own fate—Port Harcourt ensured Homicide was always busy.

I was relaxed as I went through the security check at the outside gate and then drove past the old block of offices to the newer one across the Yard. I pulled my car up within a few feet of the new building's front steps. Blocking the front steps a bit was my way of making a statement. Why use the parking lot? That was for someone else, and I was not someone else. Does that sound arrogant? I am not sure you can be a Homicide detective without some arrogance flowing in your veins.

Captain Godwin Akpan responded quite strongly the first time I parked in front. He was forced to walk around my car, which he thought demeaning. He threatened to write me up for insubordination—"the unruly act of blocking the entrance." But he only threatened. When he saw that the threats did no good, and that I continued to park in front of the stairs, he let it go. He really had no choice. I was not going to budge and he was a pragmatic fellow. I liked him, but his insistence on going by the rules always got in my way.

Akpan was a model police officer. He took himself seriously and followed his own standard of being a "good cop." He was also too self-confident and aggressive, and could be very demanding and critical. You usually knew where you stood with him. He was straightforward with his staff. Although he was often a pain in the ass, we still had a good enough relationship.

When he let it go, I responded politely: I followed the silent protocol and whenever I parked and got out of my car, I did not smile. It is not the Nigerian way to rub it in. Parking in front of the steps is one thing, grinning about it quite another. Though it might be good to try it once just to see what happened . . .

I saw Barrister Howell Osamu, of Osamu and Associates, walk out of our building and toward a new Lexus Jeep. The SUV looked like it had all the extras. Lucky man, he. Did his luck make him wealthy, or did his wealth make him lucky? Or did luck have nothing to do with it?

Quite a legend Osamu was—famous for saving Barigha Duncan from jail time. Duncan was the boss of the organized crime syndicate in Port Harcourt, the Duncan family. His mistress died in his house one night after he brought her home from a club. Word was he suspected her of cheating on him. When he confronted her, she denied it. In the ensuing discussion, she suffered massive damage to her head, which killed her instantly. Duncan was smart enough to call Osamu, a budding lawyer trying to make his mark in Port Harcourt. Osamu had already won some important cases, putting him in demand in and around Port Harcourt, but he had been waiting for the Big One, and the Barigha Duncan case was it.

The state attorney hurriedly prepared the case, assuming he'd have no problem, given that Duncan had been alone with the mistress, and she was obviously the victim of a homicide. But no murder weapon had ever been found, and Osamu had experts testify that the mistress had tripped on a settee while trying to strike Duncan, hitting her head on the hard floor. Of course, a fall like that would not cause massive skull damage, but that was where a good lawyer, in those heady heights, gets brainy. Or was it because the autopsy was conducted by someone who needed some extra cash? The autopsy did not support a murder charge, thus the opportunity to nail Duncan went down the toilet. The jury ruled it an accidental death, and Duncan walked out a free man. Osamu had won his first (but not last) truly sensational case. Suddenly, he was transported into the league of attorneys with millionaire clients. There were plenty of crooks who needed his services. It took no time at all for him to start buying very expensive new cars.

I was not surprised to see Osamu at the headquarters. He was a frequent visitor, as his clients were of the criminal persuasion. I noticed a young man with him, wearing an odd-looking trench coat and a knit cap—odd because why would he wear such heavy clothes in the heat? He looked young enough to be a college student, not more than twenty-two. His lanky frame was delicate, his clothes a bit more expensive than usual. There was a nasty scar on his right cheek. He appeared nervous, shifting from one foot to the next, avoiding eye contact with me as I looked over at him.

I wondered what the lawyer Osamu and his friend were doing here. Whom had he sprung this time?

Since I was not on greeting terms with him, I ignored him and his young friend. But I figured I would see Osamu again, sooner rather than later.

CHAPTER FIVE

I walked up the steps and into the building. Some of the officers saluted when they saw me, some waved, few stopped. I chatted with a few friends as I walked through the lobby, then took the stairs up to the second floor, preparing myself to meet Chief. By the time I stopped at the steel-framed door, I was ready. The smile on my lips was quite suitable for a mid-ranked officer, I thought. I opened the door to Chief's office and entered without knocking.

Stella, Chief's secretary, looked up from her Imperial manual typewriter as I stepped into the carpeted office. Stella was a small, neat woman. She wore no makeup, combed her hair straight—nothing fancy. My guess was she had no boyfriend—her whole life seemed to be working for Chief. She kept her distance from the men in the block.

The air conditioners kept everything cool. The more important the official, the better his air conditioners, the cooler his office. Chief of Police Isaac Olatunji was *very* important.

Stella excelled at pretending to welcome anyone who came through the door. "Good morning, Tammy."

"You look exceptionally happy to see me this morning," I said.

"With you, I pretend extra hard."

"Thanks. Is Chief in?"

"Yes, but he's with someone. You have to wait, and don't bother with your usual attempts at being friendly."

"What do you mean?" I asked, looking into her dark eyes. "When have I ever tried to be friendly?"

"Ha ha. Sit down and be quiet. I have work to do."

"Yes, Stella. Say, how did you get that name, anyway?"

"My mother was once married to Marlon Brando. Now, sit and be quiet."

I barely had time to sit in one of the comfortable chairs before Chief emerged from his office, escorting a well-dressed young man. Chief was in uniform, tall and imposing. The man wore an expensive suit and was new to me. He looked like a high-profile business executive. He was well fed, his nails manicured, his expensive shoes polished. Calluses covered his fingers but they were old ones—he had probably been a manual laborer, but at least ten years ago. Mr. Young-and-Well-Dressed seemed happy enough—he appeared to have been entertained rather than investigated. He looked like a gentleman. I liked gentlemen.

They shook hands at the door and Mr. Old Calluses left with a graceful yet purposeful walk—he was in no hurry to leave, but he was going somewhere. You could say he was none of my business, but obviously, you have never been a Homicide detective. My business is everyone. Over the past eleven years, I have always found it pays to notice details, even when you are not on a case. Mostly I look for details involving murder victims, but it also pays to keep an eye on the currently living—it saves time later, after they are dead.

Chief was aware I was there but kept watching his visitor's back until he had left the office. Then Chief pretended to first notice me, waving me to follow him as he walked back through the open doorway of his office.

"Good morning, sir," I said, closing the door behind me.

"Morning, Tammy. Femi told you I wanted to see you?"

"Yes, sir. It's a hot day."

"Don't bother. I have no time for patter today." He motioned for me to sit down, a privilege not given to most junior officers. We were chummy—to the chagrin of Captain Akpan. I am not a charmer on purpose, but Chief had always seen something in me he wanted to cultivate. I had yet to learn what he wanted to grow inside me. For now, being Olatunji's favorite made my life a lot easier. Akpan did not like the interference with the lines of authority, but he knew better than to question anything Chief wanted to do.

"I told you to have the report ready this morning." Chief held his reading glasses up to the light, rubbed them gently with a cloth, and, when satisfied they were clean, put them on and began to read through a folder on his desk, apparently ignoring me. That was typical. He was no-nonsense. I had come to deeply respect him over the past decade of working for him. He had taken me under his wing with as much affection as he allowed himself to show anyone, which was not much. He hated wasting time, and enjoyed making the point to me by usually performing two or three tasks while talking with me. Today was not a bad day—he was only reading.

"I was going to finish it when I came to work this morning."

A tiny smile on his lips, he did not look up but instead casually flipped a switch on his intercom. "Could you tell Staff Sergeant Okoro to come over?" he told Stella, then flipped the switch off and began signing papers. I waited, watching him, wondering who Mr. Old Calluses was and why Chief had seen him.

Chief of Police Isaac Olatunji had worked hard to be where he was. The man was probably one of his networking contacts. Chief was in his early fifties, tall, slender, with a long slim face. A Yoruba Moslem from the South-West, he did not indulge in smoking, drinking, or womanizing like some other officers.

"Sir, I saw you on TV yesterday on the national news. If I may butter you up, it was a fine speech. If someone had tried to kill Okpara it would be no surprise; it was one more example of the dark cave into which Nigerian politics has crawled."

He looked up at me briefly, arched his eyebrow, then went back to reading and signing. "I don't need any of your blathering today, detective. If you really wanted to butter me up you would have gotten your report finished and on my desk this morning." All while reading and signing. "I don't watch myself on television. Why were you watching it instead of working?"

His voice was hushed and serious. Chief had rung me up himself yesterday to say there had been a bomb explosion at Okpara's house, and he wanted me over there immediately. It was very rare that he would call me directly about a case.

At least he kept me working.

There was a knock on the door. Chief said "Come," and Staff Sergeant Okoro entered. Chief tore himself from his paperwork for a moment. Okoro saluted, just as a good police officer should. I respected that good-police-officer approach. I respected Okoro. He was like one of my uncles. An uncle who drank all your beer if you left him alone in your kitchen—but an uncle.

"At ease, sergeant," Chief said. "Temporarily transfer the Team B surveillance van to Akpan."

"But, sir—"

Chief raised his hand. "We have no choice. Get the van ready. He dropped by this morning to say his team needs the other surveillance van. Theirs is in the workshop again."

"Yes, sir." He saluted again, quite neatly. As he turned sharply on his heel, he shot me a despairing look. For his benefit—actually, he has to do what Chief tells him—I shrugged my shoulders at him: *What can you do?* Team B was his team but Akpan had the rank.

After Okoro left, Chief said, "The report on my desk, detective, by noon. You can go."

I said, "Thank you, sir," and got up.

"Tammy, call Stella in here on your way out."

"Was her father really Marlon Brando?"

"No, it was that Tennessee Williams fellow. You can leave now, detective. I have important things to do." He was back to the papers on his desk.

I excused myself, saluted as best I could, and left his office. Stella nodded at me as I walked by, busy at her typewriter. I told her Chief wanted her in his office and she scurried inside. I went down to my car and drove to the older block across the Yard.

When I walked into my office, I saw my partner, Femi, deep in files, almost like a younger version of Chief. He had opened the only window for relief, but the steamy air was no improvement. My office was small. No new paint on the wall, no new furniture. The floor was rarely cleaned, the windows never. Many seasons had passed since I became a detective, and my office remained as grungy as it had been when I walked in the door for the very first time.

"Good morning, lieutenant," Femi said as I squeezed past him. "Here is the final report on the bombing."

Didn't know Femi would have the report ready. Wasn't about to face Chief with the report.

I sat and opened the file but found it difficult to concentrate. I knew the details already, but the file had to be checked for accuracy. I had lost interest before I finished page ten and gave up totally at thirteen. The file in my hands, I pushed my chair back as much as I could in the space available, stretching my legs. I looked over at Femi. He ignored me, having his own work to get through.

I looked at the file but thought about Freda. I'm not a bad guy. My dog loves me—well, it would if I had one. Freda. She deserved much more than I was giving. It was a lot to live up to, and I did not know if I had it in me to give more. My work took plenty.

It did not make sense. Freda appeared to be everything I wanted in a woman. It was luck that she was not just my lover, but my friend; luck that she wanted me. Good luck for me. Whether it was also good luck for her wasn't for me to say, but I knew the answer, and I was not proud of it. I knew I had to make a decision, and that if it was to stay with Freda and meet her needs, I would have to push myself. I was used to pushing myself for work, but not for anything else.

I was attracted to her the first time I saw her, at a friend's birthday party. I couldn't help but stare. It was a combination of her stunning physical presence and her attitude. She had modellike long slim arms and legs. Her fine, short, straight sable hair accentuated her huge hazel eyes. Fair complexioned, she'd narrowly escaped being an albino, but I bet neither of her parents is. She was elegant in a black flowing dress that bared her lovely shoulders. My mind told me not to stare but my eyes would not obey.

She was chatting with our host, Modestus, and two other men. He was married, and his wife, nearby, kept an eye on them. I wondered which one of the two men had come with Freda, or whether either had, and whether I could arrest both to get them out of the picture. It never occurred to me she had not arrived with a man—at least, not until pondering it just now.

I knew I could use Modestus for an introduction to this fabulous mystery woman, especially with his wife watching. As I approached, the woman turned my way and our eyes met. I smiled, raised my glass of wine to her, and mouthed "Cheers." She ignored me. That was a good sign. She had taste, ignoring me. The two men walked off so I made my move before any other men got ideas.

At first I ignored her and greeted Modestus. "Happy birthday, old boy," I said as I shook hands with him.

"Thanks buddy."

That was as long as I could ignore her. "And who's this?"

"Tammy, meet Freda Agboke. She works with the Mercury Insurance Company here in Port Harcourt."

She held out a well-manicured delicate hand. A pianist's long fingers. Slim wrists.

"Pleased to meet you," I said. Her hand felt warm; touching it was like walking into your home.

"Freda, meet a very good friend of mine, Tamunoemi Peterside. We all call him Tammy. He's a police detective attached to Homicide. You can get along with him when he's not carrying handcuffs," he said, punching my side playfully. "Or maybe especially when he's carrying handcuffs." That was Modestus—always subtle.

"My pleasure, Mr. Peterside." Very cool. She had heard it all before. I might as well have given up and gone home if I was going to just feed her lines.

"Detective Peterside," I corrected.

"*Detective.*" She smiled sweetly, but it was not sugar I was used to. "Why are you a detective?"

I had no ready answer. My mother never understood why and my father had hated the idea. I did not even take bribes, so a lot of my uncles asked why I would be a police officer in Port Harcourt if I wouldn't profit from it. "I'm no good at conversation. So I work with dead people. I don't have to talk much with them."

Her smile changed, warming.

Modestus looked at Freda, at me, and begged his leave. Neither of us noticed.

"Are you married, Tammy?"

Well, that was direct. "No. My mother wants me to be."

"Why?"

"She thinks I'm lonely."

"Are you?"

"Not right now."

"And do you want to be married?"

"No."

Her smile grew a little warmer. "And why not?"

"In my work, I too often see the results of love. There's usually a blunt instrument involved, and a fair bit of blood."

"Maybe I should help you overcome your cynicism."

"Maybe you should."

That was exactly twelve months ago. We had gone out steadily since then. With romance, time flies—like flies on a corpse. Okay, I have not completely lost my cynicism, and I am uncomfortable. After a year, Freda wants, and should expect, a commitment.

I sat back in my office, thinking about meeting her a year ago, thinking about where we were today: the same place. I yawned and looked up at the wall clock. Three long hours to lunch.

The commitment thing was not going very well for me.

I sighed and picked up the file again.

CHAPTER SIX

It was already steamy and hot in my office when I finished reviewing Femi's report on the bombing, beads of sweat glistening on my neck. Femi was worse: the back of his white long-sleeved shirt was soaked, clinging to him. Apparently engrossed in his work, he pretended not to notice me looking at him. We both had work to finish before it got too hot to concentrate.

Femi was a quiet and reserved individual. He generally took things very seriously, but he also had an offbeat sense of humor. We got along fine, except when he sounded like Akpan; sometimes he became overly obsessed with procedure, insisting on doing everything "by the book." Me? By the book, my ass.

I read through his report. Not much there, he did not have much to work with, but the implication was clear that the bomber must have had help from the security guard at the gate: Without a friend on the inside, how else did he get past the front gate? I finished the report but it did not answer the most important questions, so I interrupted him. He would tell me what he would not put in writing. "What do you make of Okon Abasi?"

He looked up. "Who?" He looked drained from the long hours of concentration. He started earlier, I stayed later. Pity we had no laptops like police do in the "civilized" countries, where a detective's work is made easier by technology. In Nigeria, we work largely by experience, common sense, instinct, judgment—detective work. No software program to break the information into bite-size pieces, no fancy electronic gadgets to show you patterns—there is only paper, what you remember, and your intelligence to help see you through.

"The security guard at Okpara's. You interviewed him. What did you think of him?" I asked. "Does he strike you as the square and straight?"

Instead of being square and straight with me, Femi decided to wax philosophical: "How straight can one be in the face of poverty and the greed bred out of poverty?"

"Okpara probably pays him well, if only to keep him loyal."

"You'd think. But he doesn't seem to hold any leads for us."

"I'm thinking the bomber must have had help from the guard. How else did the bomber get into the compound?"

"That would be one way."

"What was it you said: How straight can one be in the face of poverty?"

"What if the bomb plot did not work—which it didn't. Okpara is still alive, he'd figure out what had happened, and the guard would not see the next sunrise."

"Maybe the guard did not think of that," I said, nodding. "Come to think of it, how much would you accept to help someone murder me?"

"It would have to be more than two weeks' pay," Femi said to me. "For enough money they could blow up the Chief, for all I'd care. I'd be long gone."

"That isn't a nice thing to say about your chief of police."

"He isn't chummy with *me*."

"Maybe whoever paid the bomber already took care of the guard. We should interview him again. In depth."

"Bring him in?"

"Yes. Meanwhile, I want to pay the Karibis a visit."

"What are you up to?"

"I want to speak to Mrs. Karibi a second time. Maybe we missed something the first time around. Maybe I'll speak first to the guard's wife. Your report has her address."

"What good would that do?"

"I want to see if the guard has suddenly come into money since his master was nearly blown to bits. Maybe we'll get lucky and find out he's bought a new TV he can't afford." I got out of my chair. "Bring in the security guard and keep him until I'm back."

Femi nodded and picked up the phone as I left. I walked outside and regretted leaving even my office; the intensity of the sun created a vapor steaming up from the nylon tar covering the courtyard floor. Nylon tar was a poor choice compared with interlocking tiles or even concrete. However, contracts are awarded not for quality of work but for who you know.

Before I saw Mrs. Karibi, or the guard's wife, I knew I first had to go up to Chief's office.

As usual, Stella was busy at her desk. She waved me in. Neither of us had the time for a frivolous chat.

"Good day, Chief," I told him as I walked in.

He looked up from his endless paperwork. "Good day to you, detective. I expected you. Sit."

"Thank you, Chief." He was not surprised. I should not have been. I sat.

"Where is the Okpara report? I'm under pressure."

"That's why I came."

"Is it? Fine. What do you have?"

"For now, only suspicions."

"Such as?"

"The security guard and how the bomber gained access."

"Are you thinking Dr. Puene?"

"Sure."

"Dr. Puene knows that he would be seen as a suspect. He's not stupid. Why would he go ahead? It doesn't make sense." He frowned, looking at me with those hard eyes.

"Maybe it isn't a question of sense. Maybe it's winning at any cost."

"Maybe he thinks he's untouchable. He has money, he's very well connected. There are lots of people who think they can get away with anything in this country so long as they know someone high up and have the money to pay." He leaned back. "Do you really think the guard was part of the plot to kill Okpara? If it failed, the guard would be the first person Okpara would look at."

"Obviously, no one thought Okpara would be alive to look at anyone."

He reclined in his chair, eyeing me as if trying to decide what to do next—and perhaps he was. I felt uncomfortable. Why was he being so sharp? What was wrong? He was silent for a few more moments, and when he did speak, he sounded resigned. "I'd appreciate it if you don't stir the hornet's nest. You're always taking chances. Your fall could well mean others will fall. Remember that."

Others. I respected Chief, but compared to me he was always the politician, always. That was why he was Chief and I was a detective. He cared about politics, I cared about solving the crime. "I'll be careful," I replied slowly.

He picked up his pen and said, deliberately, "Okay, then," not meaning it.

"A lead, that's all it is."

"If you must you must. You have my approval. Go and check out your lead. But I want the report on the bombing."

"Femi is finishing it. I'll have him send it over. Thanks, Chief." I stood to leave.

"Tomorrow morning, detective."

"More likely this afternoon."

He waved me away and returned to making notes in a file folder. It made sense he was worried. We were dealing with powerful people, powerful people perhaps trying to kill each other.

Half an hour later I was driving to the security guard's house at Marine Base. When I saw it, I knew I had not driven to a palace. Concrete, bare with no fence, the building seemed more like a small school with rows of rooms on either side of a U-shaped pattern, typical of public housing in this part of town. Judging from where they lived, Security Guard Okon Abasi and his family were not living the Nigerian dream.

A young naked girl of about six ran from behind the building, nearly bumping into me. An older girl, perhaps eleven, wearing only panties, followed her, shouting for her to return to the kitchen and to finish washing the plates.

I was embarrassed. I was not used to seeing naked or nearly naked girls. Where I grew up, in the townships, such sights were unknown. Usually, township people were rich, but my parents were simply comfortable. I was lucky. Everyone in Nigeria lived in extremes. The security guard and his family lived here, in the slums of Port Harcourt, while his employer lived in paradise, or as close as modern Nigeria came.

I called to the older girl.

"Good afternoon, sir," she said, apparently unaware her half nakedness made me uncomfortable.

"How are you?" I nodded at her.

"Fine, thank you."

"I'm looking for the Abasis. Do you know where they are?"

"That's us."

"Where is your father?"

"He's gone to work."

"Is your mother at home?"

She hesitated—a smart kid, wondering who I was and what I wanted. Before she could ask another question, I told her that I was a friend of her father's. I said I had a message for her mother. She stared at me suspiciously. I looked like a cop. My guess was Mom and Dad did not have many friends with the police.

"She's sleeping inside. Let me call her for you." She disappeared into the building, the second room on the left row, calling Mommy as she ran in, looking once over her shoulder at me.

I waited outside. Moments later, a young woman came out with the girl in tow. Both of them looked at me suspiciously. Mother and daughter for sure. "Yes? What can I do for you?" The mother was of average height and heavily built, with a dark complexion.

"Mrs. Abasi?"

"Who are you?" She revealed nothing more than she had to. Maybe her daughter told her I was police; maybe, like her daughter, she saw the law in me.

"Can I come in?"

"What do you want?"

"Police."

That was all I had to say—to some people. She did not bother to ask for my badge, stepping slightly to the left, allowing me just enough space to squeeze past her into the building. I found myself in a small room, a combined sitting room and bedroom. Through an open door, I saw another room with a smaller bed. Kitchenware was set up in the corner of the room. No TV, just a six-battery radio on top of the wooden room divider, along with books and some prized possessions (earrings).

The chairs were all rickety. I sat in one. Carefully.

She probably guessed why I was there. There was no point being coy. "I'm investigating the bomb blast at Okpara's. Where your husband works." Her facial expression did not change—a mix of suspicion and feigned lack of interest. "Has Okon told you about the blast?"

"Yes, the news's all over."

"Who wanted your husband's employer dead?"

"Papa Iniobong don't tell me much. Okon was lucky to be at the gate when it happened or . . ."—she gestured to the sky with her open palms—"I would have been a widow. Just like that. I told him to leave that place. All those big men and their big troubles, just leave it. But he won't hear."

"He didn't tell you anything else? Did anyone threaten his boss before the explosion?"

"I don't understand, sir." Now the suspicion was obvious—and the fear.

"The question is simple enough. Has anyone threatened to kill his employer?"

"How can I know about such things? Am I a big man?"

"So your husband never told you of any plot to kill Okpara?"

"God forbid!"

"Did you see him bring any strange objects home in the past few days?"

"No." The walls were completely up now; they were thick, tall, and had broken glass on top.

"Has he been behaving unusually lately?"

"No. Papa Iniobong is very, very normal."

"Are you positive?"

"I answered your question."

"He wasn't under pressure lately?"

"No."

She was giving me less and less. There was not much point continuing. "Okay. And he didn't bring home any large sums of money lately?"

She grinned, exposing perfect teeth.

"No?"

The grin stayed. I was the one expected to leave. She either was stupid or smart, maybe both. Certainly, I saw nothing to indicate she had come into a lot of money recently. But I could have her watched, have her bank records checked. "Thank you for your time, Mrs. Abasi."

"It's Matilda. And you're welcome, as long as you leave and don't come back." Same smile.

"Matilda, then. Thank you. Have a nice day."

She followed me to my car, perhaps to make sure I was leaving, and watched as I drove off. I saw her in the rearview mirror, arms folded over her chest, waiting until I was completely gone.

When I returned to our office Femi told me that Okon had been brought in and was waiting in the interrogation room.

"Excellent," I said. "I'll tell him hello from his wife."

"How did it go with her?"

"She knows something but I have no idea what. Maybe she just knows enough to tell me nothing."

"But she won't speak, eh?"

"Nothing worthwhile." I shook my head. "I doubt we'll get anything from Abasi, either."

"Well then, go ahead and waste your time interviewing him. I'll stay here to get some useful work done."

I gave him a sarcastic grin as I left our office. Femi liked paperwork, while I have always been the sort of guy who wants to shred the papers and go out into the field. This time instead of going out into a field, I walked across the Yard.

CHAPTER SEVEN

At the main building, Corporal Ogbonnaya Ubani was at the counter. I told him I wanted to see Abasi. He brought up a constable who took me to the interrogation room. Abasi was already there, and looked up as I walked in. I took a spare chair and dropped the bombing report on the table in front of him. It made a loud thump. I also pulled out a pocket tape recorder and pressed Record.

"You understand your rights?"

"No."

"You have the right to have a lawyer present."

"Am I being arrested? For what?"

"Are you willing to waive your rights?" Sometimes I found it helpful to ignore rights, something of course I'd never want done to myself.

"No. But that won't matter, will it?"

"Sometimes. Not today. Too much is at stake." He seemed confident enough. Perhaps he had nothing to hide after all. He was not insisting on lawyering up. "Do you know the man that ran from the bomb scene personally?"

"Who?"

I read from the report: "About six feet tall. Big man. He drives a white 305 Peugeot."

"That guy? He said he was the plumber, that Okpara called him over. It was suspicious, my master asking for a plumber himself."

"So you did not believe him?"

He nodded. I rather liked him. "I knew he was lying. I knew the workers who came to the house. I'd never set eyes on him before. And he was too well dressed for a plumber. But I checked inside. Stephen Wike told me to let him in."

"Wike?"

He nodded again.

"This is the truth?"

"Yes. Wike told me that they had called a plumber for the upstairs washroom."

"Was he the one who set the bomb off?"

"I wouldn't know. I was at my post when the explosions happened."

It was easy enough to check. Wike. Interesting. I got up abruptly and went for the door.

"Am I free to go?"

"Yes, thanks," I told him, and told Ubani to have him released.

I decided to be political. This whole case was political. I needed allies. I decided to call on Captain Akpan, who was waiting in his office. I brought him up to speed.

"Really?" Akpan asked incredulously. "Wike believed the guy was a plumber?"

"Maybe. Maybe he knew all along that this plumber knew nothing about faucets and sinks. I think Wike knows more than he is telling."

"Did the house need a plumber?"

"Haven't gotten there yet. I thought I'd pass this on right away."

"I appreciate that." He sat back, thinking. "There are six house helps and three relations we could question. They have already been interviewed, but without this new information."

"Femi and I can interview them."

"Good. Do that. Right away. What else?"

"I have more questions now than before."

Femi knocked on Akpan's open door. We both turned to look at him.

"One of the two mystery men at the Karibis last night was picked up by patrol officers. Thought you would want to know."

This was good news. "They're sure he's our man?"

"No one saw their faces earlier, but he was caught sneaking around the Karibi home."

"When?"

"Early this morning, before the sun was up. He couldn't give a straight story why he was in the area."

"Excellent. Where is he now?"

"Not here. That's the bad news. Barrister Osamu came and took him on bail."

"Howell Osamu? Same Osamu? I saw him leaving with a younger man when I came in this morning."

"Same. Same Osamu. Same young man. His name is Thompson. If that's his real name."

What interest would a high-end lawyer like Howell Osamu have in such a fellow? "I want to check on Osamu. I want to know what his interest is in this Thompson."

Captain Akpan shook his head. "Go after Osamu? Is that a good idea? What do we have on this guy? Nothing; just loitering. Osamu will be only too glad to chew your ass off if you make a charge against his client without any evidence."

"I'll take that chance."

"There's more," Femi said. "We received a call from Judge Karibi. I just heard."

"And?"

"Our men are on the way. I don't know the details yet. The staff sergeant passed it on."

"I don't like any of this, Femi. I'm going over to the Karibis. Do you have his number?" Femi checked his notebook and gave it to me. I dialed it on my cell. No answer.

In my car, I tried his phone again. On the third ring, it was answered. "Judge Karibi, I'm concerned about your call," I said immediately.

"Who is this?"

"Detective Peterside."

"This is Staff Sergeant Okoro, detective. Judge Karibi doesn't want to talk to anyone right now."

"Thanks, sergeant. Too bad for the judge. Put him on now."

There was only a slight pause before I heard the judge. "Detective?"

"I'm driving toward your house now. I am concerned about your call. The man found in your backyard this morning. He's on the loose again."

He sighed. "You are too late."

There was a pause, and Okoro was back. "Detective, you don't know?"

"Know what?"

"The judge's wife is dead. He found her ten minutes ago, in the kitchen."

"Murdered?"

"Definitely."

"I'll be there in a few minutes. I'm in the Rumuokwuta, round about."

"Yes, sir."

I don't like murder investigations when the bodies pile up. You have to spend a lot of time climbing over the bodies to get to the truth.

Staff Sergeant Okoro walked over as I got out of my car at the judge's house.

"When he came home nobody answered the door. He and his driver found Mrs. Karibi dead in the kitchen."

"Where's he now?"

"In an upstairs bedroom. I have an officer with him."

"How did she die?"

"Beaten. Head bashed in. The pathologist is on the way. There's more."

I wiped off the sweat from my forehead, the ever-present sweat, the ever-present heat. "More? Like what?"

"The maid was killed, too. I think she died from a hit on the head. We found them both in the kitchen."

"What does the crime scene say?" I asked as we walked into the house.

"Judge Karibi found the front door locked. The gardener said he was relaxing in the boys' quarters, listening to music on headphones. Says he didn't hear a thing. The house isn't ransacked, no signs of forced entry. Looks like they gained entry through the kitchen. We found signs of a struggle in the kitchen, a chair over-turned, and a table on its end."

I walked through the ground floor of the quiet house with him. There was blood on the kitchen floor.

"We found two distinct pairs of shoe prints in the backyard, going to and coming from the kitchen door."

If Thompson had murdered two women, chances were he had not been alone.

Dr. Lazarus Onwuchekwa, one of our pathologists, was bent over Mrs. Karibi's body, while the crime scene boys were taking photos. The doctor looked up. "Good day, detective."

"Is this how you like to start your day?"

He shrugged. "The pay is good."

I checked on the rest of the search, which had been done on the house and grounds. The front door was clean, but there was blood around the back door, and shoe prints in the backyard.

"Anyone talk to the gateman?" I asked Okoro. He shook his head. "Get him here. We need to know where he was when all this happened. And Judge Karibi's driver, too, I have a few questions for him."

I found the judge in a bedroom upstairs, sitting quietly on his bed, an officer in a chair across the room. He looked stunned. "Sorry, judge. I need to ask some questions."

He was staring ahead. "Now? Can't it wait, man?"

"I know. And I am sorry. But it cannot wait, not if we are going to catch whoever did this."

He looked at me now. It was not a look I ever wanted to see again. He did not want to say a word—but he was a judge, after all, and *knew*. "I got a threatening call in my office. A man's voice, telling me that my wife should keep her mouth closed. I told him she had already given her evidence. I was worried, so I came home early. The door was locked. That was not unusual, of course. But no one opened it, even after I knocked several times. Miriam, our maid, should have answered. I got out my keys and had my driver accompany me. At first, the house seemed abandoned. But I heard the television in the living room. I hoped Naomi had gone to the kitchen or washroom. But I found her on the kitchen floor. After that, everything was a blur. I think my driver called the police."

"Did the phone caller say anything else?"

"Just what I've told you. No name; I did not recognize his voice."

I like being tough but I could not bring myself to ask him anything else. I left him sitting quietly with the police officer keeping him company. The driver corroborated his story. The gateman had nothing to add except that he had observed a white Toyota truck driving around the neighborhood around ten in the morning. He thought they were probably looking for an address and were lost. There were two men inside. A huge guy was driving, and a younger, thin man was in the passenger's seat.

"Thompson," I muttered to myself. The gateman must have seen the expression on my face, for fear jumped into his eyes as the realization hit him: the occupants of the white truck must have been the killers. Now that this happened, he had to have been thinking he should have alerted the police about the suspicious men.

I let that sink in. He looked reproached enough to make me believe he had a lot of guilt weighing on his conscience. He huffed a sad breath and looked at the other officers standing around when I interrogated him. He must have been thinking of arrest. Poor guy. He was miserable. I left him to go find Okoro.

When I found Okoro, he passed on what the pathologist told

him. "Mrs. Karibi's throat was slashed. The maid was hit in the back of the head. Laz said she was hit in the back of her head with a blunt object. Maybe wood, he thought: round, like a small club. Hard to tell exactly what happened, but it looks like the maid was killed first, maybe right in front of the wife seeing how the judge's wife fell next to the maid, over some of the maid's blood from the head wound."

"Her death meant only one thing. She was right about the driver of the white Peugeot 305 being the bomber." I pulled out a St. Morris and lit it.

"What makes you think that?"

"She saw the bomber. And was very public about it. She was the only one who can positively identify the bomber. This was not a burglary where someone was accidentally killed. They came for her."

The case was getting complicated. I had a hunch a lot of what had happened was tied in with Thompson, and perhaps Osamu. Finding Thompson was critical, and his bail form possibly had clues. It was so much nicer when it was just politicians trying to kill each other. It was a long, thoughtful drive back to headquarters.

A half an hour later, back at headquarters, I asked for Thompson's bail form. But the desk sergeant had other ideas about the form when I approached him. He was old enough to be my father. In a condescending way he said, simply, "You might want to clear this with Chief. Howell Osamu is powerful."

"Definitely. He is the best ass-crack lawyer around. Any ass that needs a lawyer takes a crack at him."

"Just because you are a detective does not mean I have to laugh at your bad jokes." He sounded a lot like my father.

"Sergeant, I don't have to clear anything with Chief."

"Really? I love it when you talk like that. Gives me a lot of exciting yelling to look forward to."

"Are you refusing to give me the bail form?"

"You could put the entire department in trouble."

"You have a problem with my investigation style?"

"Heavens no."

"Good. The bail form, then."

"Oh yes, the bail form. One minute. Mr. Detective." He slowly—very slowly—walked to a row of old wooden filing cabinets, and looked through the recent folders until he found one. He took the bail bond form from the folder and handed it to me, accompanied by a sarcastic grin and a raised eyebrow.

There was no address for Thompson in the file—hardly a surprise. I would have to get the address off Osamu, his lawyer. I handed the file back.

CHAPTER EIGHT

A few minutes later, I was parking outside Osamu's law firm. It was a nice little hornet for the superdeluxe lawyer—a four-story modern office block. His office was the whole of the second floor, all of which was Osamu and Associates. His secretary looked up from her computer as I walked out of the elevator.

"Nice dress," I told her.

She had a smile like Dracula except her teeth were not as sharp. I decided not to bother with the charm. "I am Detective Tamunoemi Peterside," I said, showing her my badge. "I'm here to see Barrister Howell Osamu."

"One minute, please." She was wearing a hands-free headphone/mike. Classy. You don't usually see such things in Nigeria—they are expensive. She pressed a button on the intercom. "Sir, there's a police detective here."

I waited. She listened. She looked up at me and smiled as

pleasantly as she could manage. "I'm sorry, he's busy. But you can fill out the visitor's form and we can see when he's free for today."

I smiled back, already moving around her toward the inner office, where Osamu was. "Excuse me, sir, you can't go in there," but I did.

Barrister Osamu was not exactly hard at work. He sat with his feet up on his desk, watching television. He looked up with a scowl, not pleased to be interrupted with his important work. "Who the hell are you?"

"Detective Tamunoemi Peterside, Homicide, State Police."

He sighed wearily and looked over my shoulder at his secretary, who followed me in. "Carol, you can go back to your desk. Detective Peterside here won't need anything. He won't stay long."

"Thank you, sir." Carol closed the door and left us alone, after giving me a nasty look.

Osamu turned his attention back to me. "Well?"

"I have a few questions about Thompson, the young man you took on bail this morning."

"Make it snappy, I don't have time to waste."

"I'm trying. Give me his address."

"His address is my office." He looked at me more carefully. "My friend," he finally said, "I assume you know the law if you are a police detective. Mr. Thompson is my client. There are limits to what I must tell you. But, if I knew his address, I would tell you that. However, his address is my office because I do not have any other address for him."

"I'm looking for a killer."

"Excellent, that is what you are supposed to do. May I ask who this killer might be?"

"The gentleman you took on bail this morning. Mr. Thompson."

"I am not aware of a homicide charge against my client."

"There isn't one, yet."

"You must know better than to barge into my office like this. Have you been a detective very long? Do you intend to remain a detective very long?"

"I want Mr. Thompson for questioning in the murder of Mrs. Naomi Karibi. You may know her as the wife of Judge Karibi."

Finally, I had his real attention. He sat up straight. Well, it is an attention grabber for a lawyer to hear his client may have murdered a judge's wife. "Karibi's wife? What happened? When?"

"She had her throat slashed. Half an hour ago."

But he was not rattled—he was worth his fees. "First, I do not know where Mr. Thompson is. I will attempt to contact him. I'll see you next when you have a warrant. Until then, our conversation is over."

"Not so fast. Dr. Puene is your client, isn't he?"

I had to be sure but Osamu was evasive.

"I have many clients."

"Just interested. I need you to produce Mr. Thompson for questioning, counselor."

Smart lawyers pick and chose their battles, like smart detectives. "It may take a bit of time to find him. Next week, Friday. It's then that I expect Mr. Thompson will be available."

"Make him available, counselor. Here's my card. I expect a call, and a lot sooner than next week." I left him staring at my back.

I had no hard proof that Thompson was Mrs. Karibi's killer. My only rationale was based on what Judge Karibi's gateman told me, which was not much evidence. Any jury worth its salt would throw the case out the door. Moreover, Osamu would know that.

My case was further weakened by the fact that we didn't have the driver of the white Peugeot 305. As long as he had not been apprehended, we had no case against Puene or anyone else. I had considered bringing in Puene for questioning. I had not rejected the idea. I just had not yet taken the next step.

When I got back to headquarters, I reiterated my story to Chief. He was not willing to bring Dr. Puene in. He said it might have grave repercussions and he was not going out on a leg on this one without having hard evidence against Puene—namely, proof that Thompson killed Mrs. Karibi and that he was connected to the doctor. It was a waste of his time.

I returned to my office.

"What did Chief have to say?" Femi asked.

I sat down heavily on my chair and stared at the folder before me absentmindedly. "He didn't believe me."

"Perhaps if we had some proof," Femi said.

"We'll have the proof," I said, and got up. I left him wondering what I was up to.

I looked for Sergeant Okoro, to see what he'd learned about the car, but he was out. I left a message for him to call me. Within ten minutes of my returning to my office, he walked in.

"Didn't know you were back, sir. I went across the street to make a personal phone call. My minutes were very low."

Sometimes it's cheaper to use the commercial call center rather than your cell. I nodded. "Those GSM operators charge cutthroat rates. What did you get on the plate?"

He brought out his notepad. "The car is registered to one Mr. Charles Sekibo. Mr. Sekibo is a retired schoolteacher, his wife a petty trader." He flipped through his notepad. "They live at Plot 131, Old GRA." Such a feat would not have been possible a decade ago with the obsolete number plate system so he seemed pleased with himself.

"Good work, as always, sergeant. Thanks."

Okoro nodded and left as quickly as he had come in.

I looked at Femi. "Let's pay Mr. Sekibo a visit." I picked up my car keys, eager to leave our paperwork behind—Femi really had more of a taste for reports than I did. We left the building and went to my car. Femi slipped into the passenger's side, pushing the water bottles to the footwell.

It took about forty-five minutes to drive to Old GRA in the traffic. This part of Port Harcourt was known for traffic problems and bad roads. When we arrived, the Sekibos were not in their nice little suburban home. Their wards were of no help.

As we left the building, a voice behind us said, "Can I help you, officer?"

I turned and an old man peered at us from just inside of his door. He wanted to know why we were asking after Charles. He must have been watching us from his apartment.

"His Peugeot was used in a bombing," I informed him.

"Angus must have been driving the Peugeot. The old man Charles is, well, old. He doesn't drive anymore."

"Angus? Who's he?" I asked, not quite understanding.

"He has a son, Angus Sekibo. Twenty-nine-year-old university dropout. Still lives with his parents. He has no steady job. He has an Ibo girlfriend, Uloma; she works in a nightclub around Rumuola."

"This Uloma, know where we can find her?"

"She lives at number 125 on Azikiwe Road. Few blocks away."

There was nothing more he could tell us, but at least our trip had not been a total waste.

After thanking the kind old man we checked out the girl-friend. She lived in a one-room apartment on Azikiwe Road, in a two-story building some twenty years old. At the time it was built, concrete was in vogue, but now it looked old and out of place.

Before questioning the girlfriend, I decided to get a heads-up this time around by seeing if her neighbors had seen Angus recently.

A dog started barking as we walked up to an apartment below the girlfriend's. A woman opened the door when we knocked: stout, older, the type who watched everything and everyone. Good witness material. She probably made notes on their behavior and kept them in a file cabinet. Her dog was small but its bark was loud and did not stop. I glared at it and it shut up. I showed the woman my badge; she looked us over. The dog stood behind her and looked at all of us. It may have had a loud bark but now it looked ready to hide under the nearest piece of furniture.

I started with the girlfriend. My new witness was eager to provide information. "She's home right now. The girl works nights and sleeps in the day. If she leaves the house during the daytime, it's not for long. She has no friends and does not socialize a lot. But,"— her eyes gleamed now—"*but* there's this man who visits her. Tall guy. He would not pass for handsome but his clothes are good. He polishes his shoes."

I admired her eye for detail. "Is he called Angus Sekibo?"

"Don't know his name. I just watch them, I don't talk to them. They wouldn't talk to me anyway. Who'd want to talk to them? I don't like talking to my neighbors, I just watch them. Keep an eye on them. For my own safety, you understand."

I nodded. Neighborhood gossips were more useful than the neighbors who stayed behind closed doors. "Tall black male? Heavyset?"

Her eyes gleamed. She felt *very* important. "That would be him."

"Has he been around today?" Femi asked.

"No."

"Sure about that?"

She sniffed. "I take my neighborhood seriously. I would know if he visits. I know when anyone walks by. Either I see them or Sammy does," she said, nodding to the dog, which still stared at us like the stupid little animal it was. "When he comes, he never leaves until late. He plays loud music. Very arrogant man. Sammy hates him, don't you Sammy?"

"Thank you very much," Femi said as I finished my notes.

We were done with her, but she was not done with us.

"What's he up to?"

I just smiled. "Police business."

She liked that. Made her feel important. She wanted more, but she wasn't going to get it. I did not want to poison the well. Information should go only one way in an investigation—to me.

No one answered the other two doors, but maybe one alert neighbor was enough. We went up the stairs and I knocked on the girlfriend's wooden door. Seconds later, a slender young woman opened it.

"Yes?" she asked suspiciously.

"Uloma?"

"Who are you?"

"Detective Peterside, this is Detective Adegbola. State Police. Homicide."

Her whole reaction was to raise an eyebrow—just one. Maybe it was too early in the day for her. "You sure you're at the right place?"

"You know Angus Sekibo?"

Both eyebrows froze. Good sign. "What's wrong? Has anything happened to him?"

"Nothing. Yet. If we get to him first. Your friend's gotten himself in trouble with some very bad people. He helps us, we help him."

Her eyebrows became flat lines over her eyes. She thought it over. "Come in." We walked past her into the modest, airless, single-room apartment. She sat on the bed, offered me a cane chair but did not offer Femi anything. She knew who had rank.

I got out my pad. "When was the last time you saw him?"

"Friday night, four days ago. He came to the club and told me he was going out of town on business."

"What business?"

"You said he's all right?"

"No. I don't know. What business is he in?"

"What's wrong with him?"

"He was injured in an explosion."

"Injured?"

"Bleeding from the ear. Maybe other wounds. When he was last seen."

Those nice eyes grew wider. "Last seen?"

"Running from an explosion. What business is he in?"

She was shocked or at least appeared shocked. "I don't see how that can be," she said slowly, as if she did not believe it herself, and was trotting out the words on a trial run to see if we believed it.

I was getting the impression she would not tell me what business he was in—or perhaps she did not know. "Does he have a gun? Weapons? Explosives?"

"No. No. Why would he? We've been together three years. No."

"You were asked what business he's in," Femi said, trying to sound tough.

She sighed. "He's a businessman. He invests."

"In what?" I asked.

"In anything that brings him money. He does not talk about it much, so I don't ask. Trade secrets, he says."

Time to pressure her. "We're wasting time. His time. He's in trouble. We don't know exactly what he did but he was at the scene and it does not look good. Some people want him dead. Where is he? Tell me or I'll take you in."

Her eyes narrowed. "Njemanze Plot 22. He rented it just last week."

Njemanze was expensive. Was he already spending the money he had earned yesterday? I had what I wanted, unless she'd fed us a line. We got up to leave.

"Please don't hurt him," she said, hands clasped in front of her.

"You've just helped him," was all I told her.

CHAPTER NINE

It did not take long to drive to Njemanze, near Elechi Beach.

Angus Sekibo's bungalow was dead quiet. I decided not to bother with niceties like a warrant. A credit card in the door slipped the lock, and we went in. It was dark inside. Dark and quiet. Until I heard a scraping sound, coming from what was probably a bedroom. The doorway was open; a faint light shone from inside. I took my pistol from its holster as we approached. When we got to the open doorway, a tall, heavy man lunged at us from inside the room. He had a bandage around his ear. Our boy. He tried to grab my gun but never got close because I kicked him in the crotch.

Kicking an attacking suspect in the crotch is basic police technique all over the world.

He went down and Femi was on top of him as he hit the floor, rapping his gun across the back of the man's head for good luck. Our friend was unconscious but we cuffed him anyway. I stole a look at him as I took out my cell. He was bearded, tall, young, heavy-set, hardened by his years on the streets of Port Harcourt.

I got through to the desk sergeant, told him who I was, where we were, and what we had. Given we had no warrant, I fabricated a little and said he opened the front door and attacked us. It was true, except for moving the bedroom door about twenty feet forward. The suspect, being unconscious, did not dispute my account.

While I stood over the man, Femi went into the kitchen, got a glass of water, came back, and splashed it onto the suspect's head. He grunted and slowly came to. I jacked him up and pushed him against the wall. "Who paid you to bomb Okpara?"

"I want my lawyer." Now there was a surprise.

"You don't have a lawyer."

"Well, I want one."

"You'll want your balls in a minute. Shut up."

"I'm not telling you a thing. Kiss my fat ass."

Instead of kissing his fat ass, I gripped his neck and squeezed. In a moment, he was gasping for breath, cuffed hands flailing uselessly behind him. When I dropped him roughly into a wooden chair, he slumped on his left side and grunted like a wounded animal. As far as I was concerned he *was* an animal. An animal who tried to kill. An animal who would not talk.

Femi watched him sit in the chair and cough while I got two cold beers from his fridge. His taste in beer was good. I was impressed. Femi and I had nice cold ones, waiting for our colleagues to arrive. And arrive they did, within about fifteen minutes, four of them.

I stepped forward to greet them. "Detectives Peterside, Adegbola. Homicide."

"Are you here officially?" Sergeant Opuwari, the lead officer, asked as he walked up to us and shook hands.

"He's a suspect in the Okpara bombing."

"Does he want a lawyer?" Opuwari asked.

"Sure," I replied.

Opuwari grinned.

It was a jolly ride down to the Central Police Station of Njemanze. The officers at the Njemanze Police post had to put up with almost no resources and a crumbling, mosquito-infested station that had been half demolished to put up a block of fancy shops. They still did their work, though. I respected them.

Angus Sekibo was booked, allowed his one phone call, then put in a holding cell. After letting him sit for a while, I figured he was ready and approached Opuwari to interview him.

"You know I can't do that. His lawyer is not here yet."

"You want to tell Okpara you held up the interrogation of the guy who put him in the hospital and killed several of his people? Do you think this is the only attempt on Okpara we'll see? What if there's another one on the stove right now?"

"Will you take complete responsibility for interviewing him without his lawyer present?"

I nodded, and that let him off the hook. He watched as Femi and I walked into the holding cell. "When his lawyer comes, I'll make certain he fills out all the appropriate forms I can find, in triplicate, before he's allowed to see his client."

We police like to work together.

Our suspect was seated at a table, hands cuffed behind his back, looking suitably unhappy. His crotch probably still hurt, poor guy. I walked up to him and sat down. Femi stood, glaring at our boy for good effect.

Our boy glared back.

He was waiting for his lawyer, but Opuwari would guarantee he'd wait until we were done.

"You won't be looking so confident in a while," I told him. "Fifteen years for attempted murder. Another seven for possession of controlled substances. Then there's the vicious attack on me and my partner."

He said nothing.

"Talk to me now. Make a deal; it'll go easy on you. I want the big guy, not you."

I wanted them all, of course, and he knew it. "Go to hell. I'm telling you nothing. My lawyer will be here any minute. You don't scare me."

"Your lawyer will be held up. Maybe in traffic. I don't think he'll be seeing you for quite some time, Angus." He spat at me and Femi punched him in the gut. When Femi hit him, I felt a twinge of not guilt exactly, but something . . . But Meathead had killed at least two people with the bomb and probably would've killed us if he'd gotten the chance. "I want a name."

It took him a while to get his breath. "You get nothing from me."

I did not think I would, but I had to try. "Oh? How about some hair?" Femi grabbed a handful and yanked. Our suspect did not make a nice sound.

The door to the room opened and Sergeant Opuwari put his head in.

"Detective. Captain Davies wants you. In his office. Now." His face told me Angus's lawyer was here.

I nodded. I wouldn't get anything from Angus anyway. He

was more scared of his employer than he was of the police. Femi and I left him in the interrogation room and went down the hall.

When I walked into Captain Davies's office, Angus's lawyer was sitting there comfortably, a young man in a black suit, a white shirt, and a thin tie. I pretended to ignore him. "I heard you wanted to see me, captain."

"Detective, what's this talk about assassination? Why are you in my district?" The captain was direct enough. Direct enough for me to wonder if the lawyer had already paid him off, especially asking such questions in front of Mr. Nicely Dressed Lawyer. I wouldn't mind a suit like the one he was wearing, but my police salary was out of its league. He introduced himself, and I learned that he was from Osamu and Associates. Someone from Osamu's office was representing Angus?

I continued ignoring the lawyer and spoke to the captain. "It's the Okpara bombing. Our boy is wanted in connection with it. Witnesses place him at the scene."

"We follow procedure around here. We can't hold him. There's no charge yet and no warrant. I am releasing him to his lawyer here."

"He attacked two police officers. What better charge do you need?" It was easy enough to see where this was going: straight down the money-greased highway. Our boy had powerful friends.

The captain leaned back, looking carefully at me. "You didn't have a warrant to enter his house, did you? How you do it at headquarters is not how we run things here. We respect the rule of law. I need to speak with your chief. This is our jurisdiction, not yours. Wait at the front desk."

Ridiculous, but Nigerian. "Yes, captain."

We left and waited outside. Five minutes later, the lawyer

came out, his pockets looking lighter and the captain's heavier. My cell rang, a bad sign. I looked at it: Chief. He was not a happy police chief. I flipped open the cell and took the call. "What are you doing in Njemanze?" he barked.

"The Okpara case, sir. We found the suspect identified by witnesses."

"I know you are not there on vacation. But where do you get off, running out to Njemanze like a goddamn rookie?"

"Time was important."

"Get back here on the double. I will send someone to check out this Angus fella."

I disconnected the call and looked at Femi. "Well, that's that. It's back to headquarters."

"Do you think he's being protected?" Femi asked as we walked to my car. Femi has a wonderful sense of sarcasm. "Should we do something about it?"

"Sure, we go back to headquarters. I'm not ready for Chief's tantrum this afternoon."

This was when we heard the gunshots. Then a lot of yelling.

Suddenly police were running everywhere. Something had happened in the front of the building. We ran back and found a group of officers bunched around something on the ground in front of the building. The something was Angus Sekibo, with several bullet holes in the back of his head. He had been shot as he walked out of the building. Someone had solid information, to move so quickly to silence him. Someone organized. Very, very organized. Organized enough to murder someone on the front steps of this local police station, and not be caught.

Witnesses said two guys in a white Toyota truck stopped abruptly and the one in the passenger's seat brought out a gun and shot Angus.

I'd seen all I needed to. Femi and I walked back to my car.

"What are you going to do now?" he asked.

"I don't know. I didn't count on Angus becoming a dead end quite so quickly." I got my cell out of my pocket and dialed Chief Olatunji.

"Sir, it's me again."

"Yes, detective. What is it this time?"

"Angus Sekibo is dead."

"The bomber? We just spoke. What happened?"

"He was shot and killed as he left Central Police Station a moment ago. He was silenced before we had a chance to get anything out of him."

"You were damned right. I'd like a full report of what happened." The phone went dead.

I dropped off Femi at our office, then drove to Osamu's. I called Akpan while driving and brought him up to speed. I parked two blocks from Osamu's office and called his cell phone.

"I know about your client's overambitious plot to take political control of Port Harcourt," I said as soon as he picked up the call.

"What are you talking about?" He sounded truly surprised.

"Just tell him that I am going to get more proof and expose him before the primaries next week." I snapped my phone shut.

Then I waited. I had a bet with myself and won: less than ten minutes later Osamu came out the door looking worried. The doorman went ahead of him, making a fuss of opening the door to Osamu's Lexus when his driver pulled up. They drove off and I quietly followed, keeping the distance between us to at least three car lengths. After a while, the Lexus pulled off the main road and onto a side street leading to the heart of Borikiri. I slowed down, looking the other way as I passed the Lexus, and parked at the end of the street where I had a clear view of the Lexus in my rearview mirror. I got my camera from the glove compartment.

The Lexus just sat there. Osamu was waiting for someone. Sure enough, a black Ford Expedition rolled up behind the Lexus and parked. I started taking pictures. Osamu stepped out of his car and walked to the Expedition. The back door opened, beckoning him. He got in. A few short minutes later Osamu climbed out and went back to his Lexus. The Expedition started up, pulled into the street, and came toward me.

Again, I looked the other way as the Expedition passed. I managed to get a few more shots of it before it turned at the end of the street and disappeared. When I turned back, the Lexus was gone, probably having done a U-turn.

I started my car, the camera beside me on the passenger seat, next to a couple of bottles of water. The headquarters lab would develop and print the pictures for analysis. Hopefully, whoever was inside the Expedition could be identified.

I played with calling Okpara but in the end had a better idea: to leak the story to my friend, Kola Badmus, at *The Nigerian Chronicle*. I flipped open my cell. He was on my speed dial. "Hello, Kola. Working hard chasing news?"

"You can bet on it. How are you?"

"As lousy as ever. And you?"

"Can't be worse. My boss says I'm losing my touch, not coming up with enough new stories. He even suggested I take a vacation. Can you imagine?"

"Then you're in luck."

"Meaning . . . ?"

"I'm going to do you a favor. I have a hot story, about the murder of Mrs. Karibi. It's an exclusive."

His voice perked up. Exclusives always got journalists inter-ested. "What do you know?"

When I filled him in, he liked it. Liked it a lot.

Maybe a newspaper article would light a fire under someone.

CHAPTER TEN

The following morning, around ten o'clock, I walked into my office, a cup of coffee in hand. The instant I set foot in my office I sighed over how little had changed over the past ten years. For me, for Femi, for Nigeria. And for my lousy little office.

It was just as hot as it was yesterday, as hot as it would be tomorrow. I sipped some coffee, wondering whether I should just turn around and go back to my apartment. At least it had more windows than my office.

"Good morning, lieutenant," Femi said as I walked in.

"Top of the morning to you as well, Femi."

"Nnadozie from Forensics dropped off a package for you. It's on your desk. Photos, I think," Femi said.

Sweating already, I removed my suit jacket, hung it on the back of the chair, and sat at my desk. The brown manila envelope was sealed. I did not want to think about anything right now except finishing my coffee, but I cut open the envelope, and pictures slid out. Pictures I had taken of Osamu. Or at least I thought it was Howell, as I had not done very well getting his face in focus and in frame.

"Nnadozie was going out," Femi added, correctly reading the expression on my face. "He said it would be better if he dropped off the envelope because he did not know when he would be back."

"Did he say anything else?"

"He did say he was glad he wouldn't be here when you saw what a lousy photographer you were."

Okay, Osamu *was* headless in some photos—but really, is it bad to cut off a lawyer's head?

"How did it go with Osamu?"

I showed him the pictures.

"Apparently I beheaded him."

"Are you giving me a heads-up, ha ha?"

"I think we're onto something with Dr. Puene and Osamu."

"We know next to nothing."

"I still think Thompson, our murderer, is working for Dr. Puene."

"Why?"

"Because I haven't had enough coffee."

"And?"

"Osamu also has Dr. Puene as a client."

"Puene and Osamu have the power, not you. Are you ready to roll the dice? What if you're wrong?"

"If anyone doesn't like my style, he can go upriver."

"There's an intelligent response." Femi cleared his throat. He was smiling, but not very happily. "Is Chief included? What if he doesn't like your style?"

"Chief? What do you mean?"

"I mean the part where you send him upriver." He burst out laughing.

The phone rang and I answered it. Chief Olatunji wanted to see me. Immediately. I hung up and put my suit jacket back on.

"Going upstairs?" Femi asked.

"Chief requests your presence, you go."

"A minute ago, you did not give a damn."

"I don't, but that doesn't mean much, does it?"

"Take my advice. Don't give the old man trouble."

"Yes, tell me what I don't know. But what kind of career do I have to begin with? Have you looked at our office lately? What career can I have if I'm not related to the president? Or the vice president? Or the inspector general of police from my town?"

"Yes, it's all relative." Femi smiled at his little joke, but clearly my intensity—he always could see it faster and better than I could—worried him. "Take it easy, detective. Watch it. Your temper might get the better of you."

I gave him a mock salute and left. But I knew he was right.

When I walked into Chief's office, Stella did not look up. She was pretending to be busy typing, and that was not a good sign. She was my barometer, and no eye contact meant a storm.

Thinking it over, I stopped and knocked on his door. Stella looked surprised that I could behave appropriately if I really had to.

"Come," his voice called from the other side of the door.

I opened the door and stepped in. "Good morning, sir." I thought of saluting but decided against it—he would think I was being sarcastic.

He looked up at me. A file folder was in his hand. "You contacted Barrister Howell Osamu yesterday." It was a statement, not a question. "Captain Akpan has brought me up to date. Which is more than I can say for you, young man."

I realized Captain Akpan was standing over to one side. His eyes met mine without flinching.

"I did not step out of line, sir. Not at all. I had a suspect. I wanted to know his address and his attorney had it."

He flipped through the pages of the folder, exchanging a glance with Akpan. "And afterward you followed him to Borikiri, where he met with someone in a black Ford Expedition?"

I was surprised and had no quick response. Chief seemed to know everything.

"Well, detective?" he asked.

"Yes, sir. I did."

"Who was in the Expedition?"

"I don't know, sir." I felt not only challenged, but also incompetent.

"Hmmph. And why did you follow the attorney?"

"I thought there was a solid connection between the attorney and the bombing, given his clients."

"I am listening."

"Sir, if someone wanted to eliminate Okpara, it would be Dr. Puene. For reasons we all know. The guy Osamu took on bail was a suspect in the murder of Judge Karibi's wife. And Osamu is Puene's lawyer."

"Do you have any proof of Puene's involvement, detective?" Chief asked me.

"No, sir. Not yet."

"You're going after Osamu with no proof at all? That's beyond weak. We know next to nothing. Osamu is not a good person to harass. His clients include some of our most powerful individuals. If you are going to mess with him you had better be certain you can prove your case."

"Of course. You are right, sir."

"We don't know who was in that Expedition. It could have been one of his clients, it could have been his mistress. There is no way to know if it has any bearing on this case."

"Right now, no."

He rested his hands on the desk. "Right now, it's all just sounds, just you mouthing off. You can't say who was in the Expedition, much less that it was Dr. Puene. No proof of any kind. Just guesses. You do not make the rich and powerful uncomfortable unless you have a good reason."

Chief's eyes were steady.

Akpan cleared his throat to break the silence between us. "So what do you think, detective? What do you really think?" Akpan asked. I was surprised at his support.

"My bet is that Dr. Puene is our man."

"Hmmph," Chief responded. "Detective, this is the most ridiculous casework I have heard this year. You are talking about powerful, highly placed men. They do not have to resort to murder to get what they want. That is what money is for. Money works much better than murder."

He sounded confident but I did not believe him. I looked at Akpan, who did not look back.

"Chief," I continued, "the doctor wants the statehouse. You can never tell what a desperate man will do. The higher the goal, the more desperate. Governor is a high goal."

"It's a long shot, detective," Akpan said.

"Agreed. In the end, it's just a hunch," I said. Even with support from Akpan, I was alone—his support could only go so far. Whether Chief had career worries, whether he knew something I did not know—I was on my own. I turned back to Chief. "All I need to do is to get ahold of this Thompson character, sir. He'll prove me right."

"Good luck with that. There is more at stake than you realize, detective." He leaned forward, eyes grim. "There is a lot you do not know. I will not have you jeopardize our investigation into Osamu's activities with the Duncan gang."

"Investigation?" That caught me up short. "I don't understand."

"Tell him, captain," Chief said simply. He leaned back, watching me.

"Detective, we have followed Osamu's dealings with the Duncan gang for close to eighteen months now after the Barigha Duncan case. We have put a lot of resources into the investigation."

"I didn't know."

"Very few people can know. You were not supposed to be one of them. That is why the investigation has been successful— so far. The real problem is, this is not just the Okpara bombing. The stakes are high. We can't have you jeopardize our operation to break the Duncan gang by alerting Osamu in any way. If he realizes you are watching him, if you make him suspicious, his guard will be up. Even if he does not know about our investigation, our work could be lost or seriously damaged. We believe the Duncan crime family uses Osamu for their money laundering. Osamu has to be in the dark about our investigation for as long as possible."

"Detective," Chief said, his voice changing to something resembling friendly, "you are in the middle of an interagency task force operation involving the police and the National Drug Law and Enforcement Agency. We are trying to break the Duncan gang and flush out Barigha and others. Police Commissioner Ahmed Abdullah put me in charge. Now you may have put Osamu on alert, and we had to bring you in. Osamu is not to be rattled. Not now. We need enough evidence to put them all behind bars. Do you understand?"

"I do, sir, but . . ."

"No buts. Stop seeing him. You're not going to ruin a year and a half's work against these criminals by playing the hero."

"Isn't it in your operation's best interests that he thinks the police are after him—not about your investigation, but mine? Would that not throw him off?"

Akpan scratched his chin. "He has a point."

Chief chewed on it. "If I let you proceed, detective, what would you do?"

"Get Dr. Puene, using Osamu. If I get enough dirt on his hands, maybe he'll turn over Puene."

"Out of the question," Chief said after a moment. "We don't know if it'll work. Maybe he'll think you're somehow our point man on the Duncan gang. Maybe he'll shred his papers and skip town. Then our operation is in the toilet. I am not changing my plan. You've already done enough damage, just going to see him."

"If I don't see him again about Thompson, Osamu would get even more suspicious. He doesn't expect me to back out easily."

Akpan nodded in support when Chief looked at him.

"Very well," Chief said reluctantly. "But report every detail to me. And you are now part of the interagency Special Ops. You will report directly to me and no one else. No one else. Are we clear?"

"Yes, Chief. Perfectly clear."

CHAPTER ELEVEN

A few minutes later, I was out of the cool air and back into the heat, although Chief's office had been hot enough. Forty minutes later, I parked across the street from Osamu's office and went upstairs to the top floor, the envelope of photos under my arm. I walked up to Carol's desk. She recognized me and pressed a button. A red button.

I smiled. "Good afternoon, lady. Is your boss free?"

The door to the office opened, revealing an unsmiling Osamu. "Again, detective? Leave before I call security."

I smiled again. "Good afternoon, counselor. I came by to drop this off," I said, handing him the envelope.

He opened it. The photos slid out onto his open palm. He took one look and his eyes narrowed.

"Carol, hold my calls," he said.

"Do I call security?" she asked rather sweetly.

"No need for that. No need." He walked back into his office. I winked at Carol. She frowned.

I followed Osamu into his office, closing the door behind us.

"I assume the headless man is me?"

"Doesn't he look better?"

"Detective, your point is what, exactly? That I drive in my car? That I walk in the streets?"

"We know all about his plan. We know Thompson works for him. We know Thompson killed Mrs. Karibi, too. Mrs. Karibi saw Angus Sekibo. I need to find Thompson and the murder weapon; he'll be going down. Counselor, if you've moved past being an attorney and into being an accomplice, you can still save yourself. Throw in with us. Tell me what you know about the bombing and the plot to take political control of Port Harcourt."

His face went into frown mode. "I don't have the slightest idea what you are talking about." He was a bad liar, especially for a lawyer.

I leaned forward, inches from his face. "He is not a nice fellow. He's unfit to lead. It'll be partly your fault if such a man becomes governor."

"How dare you speak to me this way!"

"You don't have much choice. You have to work with me. By now, he probably knows I am seeing you. If he doesn't know, I'll see to it he does. I bet you can guess how they treat a snitch. Help us nail him. I can guarantee your safety."

"I do not need any guarantees for my safety. If you keep this up, it is you who will need protection."

"Is that a threat?"

He backed off immediately. "You are trying to blackmail me, detective."

"Sure I am. Call me. Don't wait long. You may not have long to act."

When I walked out of the building I looked up and down the road for our surveillance van. If Osamu was being watched, the van should be somewhere. I saw nothing—which probably meant good surveillance. If I were they, I would park a block or two up the road, out of obvious sight.

I got into my car and drove two blocks.

There it was, parked quietly on the street, windows dark. I imagined the boys sweating in the van, waiting and watching, taking pictures with a long telephoto lens, conducting audio surveillance, downloading it all automatically. Special Ops had resources I could only dream about.

If I could not have decent equipment or support, at least I had one advantage over the men locked in the van: for me, it was time for lunch. Let them stay glued to their telephoto lenses and wireless speakers. At least I got to be outside and enjoy good meals at nice restaurants around town. I started to drive to one as I replayed the drama in Osamu's office in my mind.

Howell was not a bad guy . . . maybe. He came across as controlled by forces he could not stop. Was he just a lawyer who had the usual guilty clients? Or was he more than a lawyer to the criminals who controlled parts of Nigeria?

My cell phone rang. I saw a number I had not seen before.

"Detective, it's Howell Osamu."

"And?"

"I'll do it."

He must have already known or guessed about the surveillance, and my visit pushed him over the edge. He had risen to the top ranks by knowing how to play the angles—so I had to be careful.

"You don't know how happy you've made me."

"I'm not doing it to make you happy, you son of a bitch."

"You don't have to call me names. How about we meet in the Pledge in an hour?"

"A public place?"

"Why not? They know we've met, and I was about to go for lunch."

"Fine." The line went dead.

Remarkably, everything was working according to plan. That did not happen often. I called Femi and filled him in.

"Sure he's not jerking your chain?"

"No, but I am sure he is a jerk."

"Ha ha."

"Look, Femi, I think I know this type. He's scared, scared enough to try and play me. You should have seen his expression when he saw the photographs. A few minutes later, he calls to meet."

"He's powerful."

"In the end, he's just a lawyer."

"Okay, so he's a weasel. But he's a powerful weasel."

"A weasel running for cover."

"Weasels can run fast. Do you really think he's been broken so easily? You might be walking into a trap."

"I set it up for the Pledge. It's a public place."

"I could watch from an unmarked car."

"Thanks. But I don't think he's moved too fast to set something up that would put me in any danger. It wouldn't make sense to do anything to me, anyway. I'm just one more cop. I think he's wanted to do this for a long time. Maybe he's been disgusted with Puene but can't help himself."

"Now you're back to his being a lawyer."

I called Chief Olatunji next. He answered almost immediately, as if he'd been watching his phone. "Yes?" he asked quietly.

"Sir, I've just seen Osamu. He's on board. I'm meeting him at the Pledge in an hour."

"Good work, detective. I'll have Okoro and his team in position before Osamu gets there. I'll be here if you need me. Make sure you call after you meet with him."

"Thanks, Chief. I'll call as soon as I finish talking with him."

"Fine. Get to work."

I took a drink from one of the bottles of water in my car and started toward the restaurant, planning to get there first, before anyone else could set up a trap. Maybe I'd even get something to eat first, perhaps pounded yam and bitter leaf soup.

Pounded yam is prepared from yam tubers, a perennial root crop in Nigeria. You first peel and wash the yam, then cook it until it becomes soft, after which you pound it in a mortar carved from wood. You swallow it with soup made from bitter leaf vegetables, palm oil, smoked fish, and beef. It is a major meal around here, a delicacy enjoyed in Nigeria, especially southern Nigeria.

The restaurant was not busy yet. There were some free tables in the executive suite, the side of the restaurant with better air-conditioning. It was more spacious, more exotic, more money. I took a table in the common area close to the bar, secluded but with a good view of the entrance and the other tables.

I ordered some food while I settled in. It was lunchtime. The restaurant was about half full, with mostly bank execs, business-men, wealthy traders, one or two university boys. My order came: pounded yam and bitter leaf soup with smoked fish and beef. I still had almost half an hour before Osamu arrived. The waitress did not bring the liquid soap and paper napkins, so I asked for some. When it came, I washed my hands and then ate, using my hands.

A few minutes later, and earlier than I expected, Osamu showed up. He had not used his car, arriving instead in a taxi. He stepped out of it and turned around to pay the driver when a white truck stopped ten yards away. I could not see them clearly through the restaurant window, and certainly did not see their guns—but the gunshots I heard loud and clear. Four shots, two quick ones each from two guns. Bang bang, bang bang. Not very loud. Then they were speeding away, already gone amid the street traffic and pedestrians, no one stopping them.

By then I was running out of the restaurant, my pistol ready, but the assassins were gone. Osamu sat slumped on the ground, briefcase on the sidewalk next to him, clutching his chest and spitting blood, looking surprised. Very surprised. Two rounds had missed him, but he had not been so lucky about the other two.

The taxi driver came out of his car, shouting hysterically. I told him to call an ambulance while I knelt by Osamu. I opened his case and used some of his legal papers to stop the bleeding, not very well, but then there was not much to do for him. He was already pretty dead.

"You've got me killed, detective."

"Hang on. The ambulance will be here in a minute."

"I won't make it. Tell my wife, tell her, oh the hell, don't tell her anything."

"You're not going to die."

He coughed up some blood.

The surveillance van screeched up and Akpan jumped out with two officers.

"Did you see the shooters?"

"We got some photos. We were on the other end of the street. Two cars are after them right now."

Osamu gripped my right hand. I bent forward, leaning my ear close to his mouth. He whispered an address and said "Thompson." After that, he had nothing left to say—forever.

Akpan removed his cap and wiped sweat off his face. "You hurt?"

"No. It's not my blood."

"What did he tell you?"

"Thompson's address." I gave it to him.

It took about ten minutes for the ambulance to arrive, which was about nine minutes too late.

"First, Mrs. Karibi. Then, Angus Sekibo. Now, Howell Osamu," I said to Akpan. "Sorry about your investigation."

"The Duncan family's obviously rattled. This was their handiwork, I'm guessing."

I was certain that Puene had stopped Osamu from giving him out. I did not believe that the Duncan gang had killed Osamu, as Akpan suggested.

By now, a police cordon was going up. Akpan called Forensics and was waiting for Nnadozie and his boys to arrive. I didn't tell him where I was going. As I drove off, I hoped that he did not tell the surveillance team to follow me. As soon as I was out of sight, I accelerated toward Borikiri, the waterside area, where Thompson lived.

We nicknamed Waterside "New York"—it ran over with vice and crime, thieves and pickpockets, armed robbers and thugs. The street is their home. Ten-year-olds in Waterside will sell you any controlled substances you can think of.

I pulled up across the street from the address and just sat for a while in my car, waiting. It was hardly wise to simply ask for him—the locals were suspicious of any strange face, and double for me, a police face. How they saw it I do not know for sure, but they did, and without looking twice. On the other hand, only sitting there was also generating suspicion, like sitting with a mask on my face saying "Cop looking for someone, go tell your friends." I drank some water, resisting the urge to go inside the apartment house to look for him. It was about then that I saw the same young man in an odd trench coat and knit cap, just turning the corner and coming toward me. Thompson.

He checked out the area, not yet seeing me, and began walking toward his apartment block. I slid my pistol from its holster, taking the safety off. He walked about thirty feet to the front of my car and started across the street. I waited until his back was to me and then got out of the car, pistol leveled at him.

"Hey. Thompson." He slowed but did not break his stride, as he slowly looked over his shoulder at me. "Police."

He stopped looking and started running.

My gun was useless—there were too many people around to risk a shot. I took off after him. But he was in better shape than I was. By the third block I was starting to pant. He jumped over a fence around a back alley. I followed, but not nearly as well, twisting my ankle. Concrete chips from the wall behind me hit my shoulder before I heard the gunshot. Fortunately, he tried only one round before turning, disappearing into the alley and, doubtless, out the other side within the next minute. People ran, screaming. Thompson was gone. I was left with no suspect and a stabbing pain in my ankle.

As I drove home, I thought about Okpara's personal aide, Stephen Wike. That was something I should be digging into. Wike had not acted quite right. He might be hiding something, and I wanted to find out what he knew. Certainly there was the strong possibility that an insider had played a role in the Okpara bombing. I'd already ordered Femi to check on Wike's phone records over the past two weeks. I was almost certain Puene bought him over. After what Okon told me, if there had to be a turncoat in Okpara's staff, I had a feeling it was Stephen Wike.

CHAPTER TWELVE

The following morning, I pulled up close to Wike's home and watched comfortably from across the street. I sat in the car, waiting and chain-smoking during those five long hours as the hands of my watch crawled round to 11:00 A.M. Stephen did not come out of the house in all that time. Had he spotted my car parked across from his home?

The five-hour wait had me so upset, I very nearly gave up on ever finding out what Stephen was up to.

Another hour later he finally emerged, in casual wear. He got in a car, and I followed him to the small Kumar Department Store. The store was owned and run by an Indian and his wife. The Kumars had pretty much anything you could think of: merchandise as tiny as toothpicks or as big as bicycles, all at the lowest prices in Port Harcourt. You had to wonder if the Kumars made any profit.

Most of the other stores, owned by local people, did not appear to appreciate the importance of low prices. They all wanted to grow rich overnight, so they charged more, had fewer customers, and never became rich, overnight or otherwise.

Wike walked in to the store. It was large enough for me to follow him, keeping out of his sight. Mrs. Kumar came over to greet me, sweetly cheerful as usual.

"Hello, detective. Fighting the good fight?"

"Always. How are you? How is Sunil?"

"Fine. He went out. And you?"

"Doing well."

"You've not been coming to our store lately. Tell me that any shop is selling cheaper and we'll cut our prices, just for you."

"I can't get a better price. It's just work. Too many murders. No time for shopping."

"Good. I don't like cutting prices any more than I already have. Okay, so what do you want today?"

"I've got a list in my head. I'll just look around."

Chitchat used up and over, she gave me her most charming smile and excused herself to attend to the next customer.

Keeping in between shelves, and with an eye on Wike, I picked up some odds and ends that I didn't actually need. Wike was not meeting anyone; he just appeared to be shopping. When it looked as if he was close to done, I took my basket to the salesclerk. I wanted to leave before him, to keep a better eye on him when he came out.

The salesgirl rang up everything in my basket. My bill was N1520. I paid and admired her smile as she placed everything into two brown paper bags. I should have been thinking of Freda, not her. I walked outside, unlocked my car, and put the paper bags in the passenger seat, next to the bottles of water. My cell phone rang as I turned a little to see if Wike had come out yet. The call was from Freda. Was her network so extensive that someone had already told her about my eyeing the woman in the store?

"Hello, darling," Freda said.

"Hi. I'm at work right now."

I was trying to concentrate on the conversation and to think what to say next when I saw Thompson.

For about a minute, I froze. Seeing Thompson, I knew Wike was the inside man for Puene as I had suspected. I bet they set up rendezvous like this one often and Wike would pass information to Thompson to pass on to Puene, and back. Puene dared not contact Wike on the phone or otherwise. But what I didn't yet understand was what made Wike do it: betray Okpara.

"Are you with someone, Tammy? You sound distracted. Is she so pretty that you can't take your eyes off her?"

Thompson was across the street. He did not see me. I moved behind a street pole. "No, honey. Only you can have that effect on me. You know that, don't you?"

"Hmm."

I switched the phone to my other ear. Wike had come out of the store. He was on the other side of the street, slowly walking toward a spot maybe fifty feet to my right, clutching nylon bags of junk food in both hands. Thompson was moving slowly.

"Tammy? Hello?"

"Sorry. Working. Watching someone." The street was very crowded. I did not like this.

"Who?"

"Okpara's personal aide. I met him during the bombing. I

don't like the guy and I figure maybe he knows something about the bombing."

"Should I hang up?"

"Not yet. Uh, no. I need to look like I'm doing something other than watching him."

"Thanks. Glad I'm useful."

"Sorry." Still watching Wike. He was nearing a parked car, struggling with the weight of the bags while reaching for his car keys. Thompson, tall and gangly, was now walking purposefully toward him. And he took a .22 from his pocket.

I flipped the cell closed and pulled out my police special. "Police!"

Wike and Thompson both heard me. Wike looked at me, then started to turn to see what I was looking at. He never saw Thompson. In a moment, Thompson had put four rounds into Wike's chest. Two nylon bags of junk food fell to the street. Red appeared all over Wike's shirt. He fell back against his car.

People started to scream. Thompson was already running, into the crowd.

Thompson? Wike? No choice. I rushed to the victim, who was slowly slipping to the street. His shirt was very red now. I caught him, let him down gently. His eyes were glazing over. He never had a chance.

I flipped open my cell and speed-dialed. "This is Detective Peterside. Civilian down. Gunshot, multiple wounds. I need an ambulance at 56 Orominike, outside the Kumar Department Store." It was already too late, Wike was as good as dead. I looked in the direction Thompson had run off, but there was no point in searching. He could have gone in any of a hundred directions, ducked into a hundred alleys or shops—assuming that he did not have a car around the corner waiting to pick him up. I speed-dialed again and gave headquarters a heads-up on Mr. Out-on-Bail, then leaned against Stephen's car, looked down at his lifeless eyes, and pulled out a cigarette.

A police siren came closer, then several. Soon there were plenty of cars, all too late. Uniformed police officers began to secure the scene, putting up a rope to block off the growing crowd of onlookers. I flicked my cigarette and watched the ashes fall to the ground in the dead hot air.

My cell rang. I looked at the screen. Freda again.

"Honey?"

"Yeah."

"Why did you cut the line like that?"

"I have a situation."

"I hope you are not the situation."

"Not this time. All I did was stand there. I'll call you back. I'm sorry."

"Okay, I . . ." Her voice trailed off, she could think of nothing to say; my tone was a closed door. "Bye. For now."

"Sure."

The forensics van carrying Nnadozie and his crew drove up, followed almost immediately by Captain Akpan. A dead Wike was a big deal. Femi was in Akpan's car. They walked over to me while Nnadozie and his forensics unit started unloading their equipment.

Akpan looked at me as I took a drag. He did not like smokers. "What happened?"

"I was shadowing Stephen Wike. He came out of the store over there. Thompson was waiting for him."

"Damn."

"Yeah. Thompson pulled out a .22 and emptied half a clip into him. He disappeared into the crowd."

Akpan turned away and got out his own cell phone, made a call and started giving orders. When he was done, I said, "Thompson has to work for Puene. There's no reason for him to be running around killing Okpara's people on his own. Unless he has a very odd hobby."

Akpan nodded.

CHAPTER THIRTEEN

Femi and I then drove back to headquarters in my car. I wrote up a statement, then went up to see Chief. Stella let me in right away. Chief was sitting behind his desk, on the phone. He finished his conversation quickly when I came in.

"Chief, I want to bring in Dr. Puene for questioning in the Okpara bombing and today's shooting of Okpara's assistant."

He eyed me warily. "Are you out of your mind?"

"I think he's a key player here."

"I don't have to tell you he's a powerful man."

"Then why are you?"

"Am I supposed to laugh? Is there something here that amuses you? Mrs. Karibi is dead, Angus Sekibo is dead, Howell Osamu is dead, too; now Wike?" He leaned back. "You're on dangerous ground."

But he did call Police Commissioner Ahmed Abdullah, to get

his okay to invite Dr. Puene into headquarters to answer some questions.

I went back to my office, got Femi, and we drove out to Dr. Puene's house. We found him in the same room as four days ago. An assistant remained hovering in the background.

"Good day, sir."

His eyes had the same wariness Chief's had, but some of his earlier arrogance was gone. "Yes?"

I had plenty of ways to say it. "Doctor, we'd appreciate it if you came downtown with us for a while."

"For what?"

"Just some questions."

"What about? This does not have anything to do with Okpara . . . does it?"

"Sort of. Stephen Wike was shot to death about an hour and a half ago."

"Which station did you say you're from again?"

"State Police Headquarters. Homicide."

He picked up his phone and punched in a number. If I was lucky, he was calling his lawyer. I smiled. I didn't think so. Osamu was dead.

"This is Dr. Puene. Yes. Good afternoon, Isaac."

Femi and I exchanged looks. He was calling Chief.

"Some of your detectives are here. Yes. Yes. They want me to come in for some questions." Pause. "I see. Yes, of course." He hung up. Smiling. He turned to his aide. "I'm going down to police headquarters with the detectives here. I'll be back soon."

"Are you sure about this, Doctor?" the assistant asked.

"It will be fine. I'll be back soon. Just postpone my appointments."

The ride back to headquarters took about fifteen minutes.

The good doctor did not ride with us, of course. He was driven in his Toyota Limited SUV. When we got to the station he acted more like a visitor than a suspect, and everyone but myself and Femi treated him that way. As we came in, one of Chief's assistants met us—he'd been waiting patiently—and took Dr. Puene, Femi, and me straight to a conference room. He told us to wait for the police commissioner, the area commander, my captain, and Chief himself.

I was starting to get a good idea of why Dr. Puene was smiling. Not that I had not already guessed. I told Femi to go back to our office. If I was going to shoot myself in the foot there was no point dragging him down with me.

I felt like lighting another cigarette. I don't enjoy smoking that much, but it gives my hands something to do, and by putting something in my mouth I'm not as likely to open it as much. The area commander arrived first. He smiled grimly at me and nodded at Dr. Puene. Then Chief and Akpan came in. Now we were all together. The good doctor sat at the far side of the table. He looked calm, his custom-made suit without the slightest wrinkle.

The police commissioner arrived at last. Ahmed Abdullah was as tall as Dr. Puene, largely built, with dark coarse skin, a rounded fleshy face framed with glasses, and a neck as thick as an ox. Probably with a brain to match.

His protruding stomach tugged at his crisply ironed uniform, threatening to dislodge the shiny brass button there. A very harsh man, bad tempered. Officers in the state had a morbid fear of the man. You should—if you want to remain on the force.

He and Chief greeted one another in the Moslem fashion.

I saluted.

We all sat down.

Commissioner Ahmed sat opposite Dr. Puene. To his left, from

Area Command, was Jonathan Amadi. To his right, my chief of police, Isaac Olatunji. Captain Akpan sat to his right. I sat near no one. None of them looked at me.

The commissioner spoke up first. "Dr. Puene, first I want you to understand that you are not under cross-examination. You are not under any obligation to answer any questions." The good doctor said nothing. I muttered something to myself about sacred cows. The commissioner continued, "But to see justice served, of course we expect you will fully cooperate."

"Of course," Dr. Puene said quietly. He sat back in his chair.

It was Amadi's turn. "Doctor, of course you know that anything you do tell us could be used in a court of law. Do you wish to have an attorney present?"

"Do I need one?"

They all smiled at him. No, he did not need an attorney.

My mentor, Chief Olatunji, leaned forward. "Dr. Puene, do you know Okpara?"

"Of course. He's a friend and party member. He's running against me."

Chief cleared his throat, going through the motions. "What is your relationship with him?"

"We're politicians running against each other. But we're also members of the same party. Some of our supporters do not quite get along as well as they could, but he and I are fine."

"So your relationship with him is cordial?"

"We are running against each other."

"Answer the question directly."

"I don't have to agree with his opinions to be cordial."

Puene loved to play people's feelings. There was nothing satisfying about his answers to the questions. I usually have less respect for people who are not able to stand up to someone like

Puene, and there weren't too many people in this room who would go up against him. He knew it, and he was enjoying it. So it felt right to put a damper on his enjoyment—and, well, perhaps my career did not mean all that much to me. "Doctor, do you want to be the governor of Rivers State?"

They all looked at me. I was speaking out of turn.

"With the help of God and your vote, yes, detective."

"Don't you have the best motive to blow him up? To have his assistant killed?"

His eyes grew harder than the bullets that killed Wike. He looked directly at Chief. "There is no need to be rude. I don't have to answer this nonsense. I am a highly placed and well-respected party member. That question was . . . inappropriate. I will defeat Okpara politically, you know; I hardly have to kill him."

Chief's eyes narrowed as he turned to me. "Lieutenant, proceed with caution. This is an inquiry, not a trial."

I nodded. "Of course. Doctor, are you aware of the plot to assassinate Okpara?"

"I am not aware of any such plot."

"Doctor, there is a man we know of as Thompson. Do you know him?"

"I do not know anyone of that name."

"Fine. Did you have Thompson, or whatever his real name is, kill Stephen Wike?"

"Detective!" the commissioner barked. He went so far as to remove his glasses. "You either behave yourself or I'll remove you from this panel."

I met his stare but nodded in respect. "I am just doing my job."

"Are you?" He turned to Captain Akpan. "Do you usually tolerate such an approach from a junior officer? Perhaps I should look into this personally." He put his glasses back on.

Clearly if I said anything else, I'd be thrown out of the meeting and probably get suspended. I leaned back and closed my mouth. I'd given the doctor the message. And it felt good. I could stop. For now.

Unfortunately, for my sense of self-satisfaction, the doctor looked rather amused. He could afford to be. There was no danger to him in this room, except from me . . . the "junior officer."

"Anyone with more questions?" the commissioner asked.

No one had any. What a surprise.

The doctor smiled. "Every opportunity I have, please believe that I urge my supporters to desist from violence. Yet, there has been violence. For example, at the peace meeting we had, there was an unfortunate incident. But both Okpara and myself believe in the democratic process. We know that violence is a cancer. That is why we want to change things around."

Good political speech, I thought.

"Thank you, Dr. Puene," Captain Akpan said, smiling.

The commissioner joined in. "Doctor, thank you very much for coming today. We have no further questions." He started to pack up his papers.

That was it. We all stood. They shook hands. No one shook my hand. The good doctor smiled at me and left. They all walked out, leaving me alone. I looked down at the table. Chief came back into the room a moment later.

"What the hell were you doing?"

"What you taught me," I replied, trying to look puzzled.

"Knock off that look with me. You were way out of line. Why ask him such obvious questions, unless you just wanted to provoke him?"

"Would we not have looked foolish if no one asked him a hard question? At least now we can say we tried."

"You did not ask him any hard questions. You only embarrassed yourself." He looked at me, trying to figure out if I was being sincere or sarcastic. "I don't have the authority to cover you if you persist." He turned on his heel.

I was left alone in the conference room, and eventually walked out by myself.

CHAPTER FOURTEEN

When I walked into my office, Femi looked up from the report he was writing. All he needed was a glance. "I see it didn't go well."

I sat at my desk. A draft report on the Wike murder faced me.

Femi was still looking at me, wanting more, so I told him, "I figured I didn't have much of a career anyway. It's good you weren't there. Will you give me some money when they fire me?"

Femi laughed. "You got nothing out of him?"

I shook my head. "Without evidence, all I could do was bluster. And no one around the table was interested in my trying to pressure him. He's too high up. Maybe I'll give up police work and write a novel."

Femi was used to my moods. I had started out idealistic but life has a way of changing that.

Akpan startled me, coming by my office a few minutes after, to tell me that a gunshot had been reported at Borikiri, around the time I left yesterday. He pointed out that the shooting was near the reported address for Thompson. "Bystanders told us that one man, about your age and height, was chasing a younger man who fit Thompson's description. Some coincidence, eh?"

We exchanged a look. "Any news of Thompson's whereabouts now?"

"I have officers working on that. They have orders to bring him in alive. And they are in good enough shape to run him down if he tries to get away." He smiled flatly. Or was it sarcastically? "Just thought you'd like to know."

I was thankful he was on my side. He could have been upset.

"And, Chief wants to see you."

"About what?"

"He did not bother to tell me. It sounded . . . urgent."

"I hear you. I'm going right now."

I stared at the open doorway after Captain Akpan left, thinking over what he said.

At Chief's office, Stella was in the front office as usual, typing away on her old Imperial manual.

"How are you?" I asked.

"Don't bother with the repartee, I'm busy."

"I'm here to see Chief. Is he free?"

She nodded. "He knows you're coming. Just go in. I know what you're going to ask, so don't bother. I don't know anything."

I asked anyway. "What's happening?"

Stella frowned and did not look up, avoiding my eyes. Not a good sign.

I walked into Olatunji's office. He looked up with displeasure. Another bad sign. Today was not to be a chummy day.

"Good day, sir." I walked up to his large desk.

He had his speech ready and did not waste time. "We worked

the interagency operation for eighteen months. Now Osamu is dead. And this afternoon was the final nail in your coffin. A number of people want you off the case, and I can't disagree. That's the best I can do to appease them." He said it crisply. I don't think he wanted to say it, or at least I did not want to think he wanted to say it.

"I don't understand."

"That's just it. You do not understand."

I looked at him directly. He looked back more so. "Tell me this is a joke, sir."

He got up from his executive chair and walked to the window, his back to me, hands in his trouser pockets.

"It is no joke," he said quietly, looking out the window.

"You're going to let some brass-button hound you into doing this? Take me off the case in the middle of an investigation into multiple murders?"

I had every right to be angered by his decision to pull me off the Okpara case.

He turned, looked at me angrily, then returned to his executive chair. "I told you. It was not my decision. You ask why you've been taken off the case? That you have thrown caution to the winds is more than enough reason. I tried to slow you down and you ignored me. You're an ingrate. I am disappointed in you, Tammy."

I was completely taken aback by his anger. I did not know what to say—anything would be wrong. So I just nodded, accepted his summary dismissal, and left. In the outer office, Stella kept her eyes down as I went by. "Duck," she told me under her breath.

As I walked through the lobby, the boys at the counter eyed me jealously because they thought I had Chief's ear—they had no idea what was really going on. I nodded to their salute and left the building.

I needed to see what my options were, and make some private calls. My office phone could be monitored if I was under surveillance so I walked to the phone booth across the street, dialed our Area Command, and prayed that I would get Amadi directly. He answered on the fourth ring.

"Yes?"

I was nervous. This was not the sort of thing I'd ever done before. "It's Tamunoemi Peterside, sir."

"What a pleasant surprise." From his tone of voice, he already knew, but I went through the motions anyway.

"Will you speak to Chief Olatunji?"

"No. Frankly, Tammy, this one is beyond me. There's nothing I can do here."

Right. "I can't quit this or be put off. I'm working something big here. Dr. Puene is involved. This could be what we've been waiting for. We could finally get something on him."

"Whoever said we wanted to get something on Dr. Puene? Who is this 'we'? I can't help you."

"You don't understand."

"Sure, I understand. So do you. Listen. How shall I put it? Hmm. How about this: You've gone out of your mind."

"I'm just doing my job. A lot is at stake here."

"You are certainly right about that." The line went dead.

I lit a cigarette. I did not like the taste but drew the smoke into my lungs anyway. Breathing the air was as deadly as smoking anyway. Life can be like that.

I thought longer about who to phone next. This time, the police commissioner.

"Yes. I know why you're calling. Don't bother asking," he said.

"Ask him to put me back on."

"And how would he do that? And why would he listen to me? Sorry, Tammy. Chief Olatunji is under pressure and he made the decision he had to make. That is his job. I trust his judgment."

"Even when it is obvious something is wrong?"

"Especially when it is obvious there is something wrong. That is why I delegate. Take some good advice, Tammy. Don't call me again, and don't call anyone else." The line went dead. Again.

I needed a break. All of a sudden, I wanted to talk with Freda. Maybe that was a good sign. I called her up and she made time between her appointments. She was waiting outside her office building when I drove up. Her smile was almost as hot as the sun. She walked over to my car doing interesting things with her hips. It was hard to keep my eyes off them, and it appeared she did not want my eyes off them. She smiled. Her manicured fingers had long blood-red nails.

As we drove through Rumuokwurushi, she chattered away, talking marriage, or about her friends, all of whom happened to have already gotten married. She was counting them off on her fingers. She had a lot of fingers; it seemed she was the only one left. I got the message. Call me Mr. Insensitive, but right then it did not feel like a marriage discussion kind of day.

Freda had wanted us married ever since we met. I was not sure why, or why I was seeing her right now. But here we both were. Weren't we?

"Did you hear what I said, Tammy?"

"Everything."

"About Rebecca?" she asked.

I sighed. "She's getting married. I'm happy for her."

"When are you going to get serious?"

"Seriously, I'm happy for her."

She looked at me, really looked at me, for the first time. "What's going on?"

"Don't you think the weather is very hot today?"

"Tell me."

I found a quiet, isolated place, pulled the car over, and killed the engine. There was a pause.

She finally asked, "How are you getting on with the case?"

I took out a cigarette. She did not want one. I lit it and blew the smoke out the window. I hated to cast a shadow over her happiness but I had to tell her anyway.

"I've been pulled off the investigation."

She was surprised. I usually don't talk with her about problems at work—of course, mostly there hadn't been any serious problems at work. "Why would they do such a thing?"

"It's internal." I was not sure how much to tell her. For that matter, I was not sure how much I knew myself.

"So what will happen now?"

"They're putting another detective in charge."

"There is nothing you can do?"

"Good question." I concentrated on my cigarette.

"Why would Chief take you off?" I said nothing. "Tammy, cut this and talk to me."

"Chief said I was reckless. That I don't follow procedures. That's all I know right now. But it is not the whole story. Something much larger is going on."

"Isn't Chief your friend? Can't you just talk to him?"

"Not anymore." I looked at Freda. "It's smoke."

"Smoke?"

"Politics."

"But is it true you didn't follow procedures?"

"Well . . . well, yes."

"Why wouldn't you follow the rules? Are you trying to wreck your career? What's wrong with you?"

"All that was wrong with me is that I was doing my job."

"I don't understand you at all."

"Me neither."

I threw away what was left of my cigarette and started the car. "I'll drive you back."

"And?"

"I don't know."

She said nothing all the way back. At her office building, she got out of the car and went inside without looking back. I watched her get smaller in the rearview mirror as I sat inside my car for a while. Just sitting there thinking was frustrating.

I drove back to my office. I was sulky all afternoon.

CHAPTER FIFTEEN

The phone rang. I asked Femi to answer it and he picked up the receiver. "Homicide. Detective Adegbola." He listened, then turned to me. "You in?" he mouthed.

I shook my head. "Sorry, he isn't." After listening some more, he cupped the mouthpiece with his palm. "You want this one. It's the doctor."

"Puene?"

Femi nodded.

"He wants me?"

"No one else."

I sighed but nodded.

"Wait one moment, Doctor. I see him coming in."

I picked up the phone after a moment. "Detective Peterside." I was not surprised when the good doctor invited me to his home to talk—privately—about something bothering him. Could I come right away?

Why not?

It did not take long to get to the doctor's place. Traffic was light. The same uniformed guard as before opened the gate. He was expecting me. He stepped aside to let me drive in and I parked in front of the main house. I ignored the usual people hanging around outside as I got out of my car. Before I could take a step, the doctor's assistant came out of the house: "He's waiting for you."

I followed him inside, where my host was waiting. He stood as I walked in. The atmosphere was pleasant enough, considering two hours ago, I had rudely accused him of murder. He had changed into a more Nigerian outfit, a full-length dashiki in blue cotton fabric and pants that had matching embroidery in gray. He looked casual.

"Good day, Doctor."

"And to yourself, detective. Please. Sit."

I sat on an expensively padded settee, ready for whatever the doctor wished to dispense.

He wished to dispense an intoxicant. "Drink?" he asked as he walked to the bar.

"I don't drink on duty."

"All the other officers who've visited have had something to drink."

"Well, then, it's up to me to maintain our false image of being sober at work."

"I'm impressed. I am, detective."

"Thanks."

"You are most welcome."

He poured himself a drink, a small one, then moved toward

the window, sipping and looking down at the supplicants and hangers-on. He sighed. "Did you see all these people?" he said. "They don't care if I win or lose. All they care about is my money. Everybody wants my money." He turned to face me. "Have you thought of running for political office?"

"No. We are not allowed to."

"You are better off. Politics is such a dirty game in this country. It is a dirty game to begin with, but here you feel the mud. It gets between your fingers."

"So why not get out of it? You're a doctor. You could be saving lives."

He waved his hand, holding the glass, at imaginary foes. "Someone's got to stand up to all this. Is that not using some of your own words, detective?"

I leaned back. He could certainly be charming enough. "You said you want to talk about something that's bothering you?"

"Yes. I expect I shall have some sleepless nights over it." What he said next sounded rehearsed. "Detective, someone wants me dead. I'm worried sick about my safety, now that the primaries have heated up."

"I thought we were going to talk about Stephen Wike."

"We are. I was shocked when I first heard. Now I've had time to think."

"Why are you shocked? Did his murder not follow naturally?"

My question did not faze him in the slightest. He finished his drink. "You really think I did it?"

"At the very least, you know more than you are telling. You and Okpara are at each other's throats. Everybody thinks you ordered the bombing and this hit."

"Do they? Why would I order the killing of Okpara's personal aide?"

Then, he said something I had not expected. "Five days ago, my mechanic checked my gearbox and axle oil before we were to drive to a meeting with elders and traditional rulers, and he found a bomb had been planted under my car. I called the police but it was kept very quiet. The bomb squad took care of it. Naturally, I suspected Okpara. Until someone tried to blow him up. Now I have no idea who to suspect." His grim expression appeared real. "Detective, a third person wants both Okpara and myself dead."

"And what did my colleagues say?"

"The colleagues who were around the table today? They say they are investigating. I don't believe them, and from your expression during the meeting, I do not think you believed or trusted them, either. You think they are not interested in investigating me. You are right, detective. They are not. But not because they are protecting me. There are many games being played out." I was leaning forward now. Very good—this was not what I had expected at all. "So, detective, what should I do? Wait until someone succeeds in killing me?"

Was he playing me or was I playing him? "Perhaps you should do nothing. I need some time. Are you sure you can't talk to Olatunji?"

"I can ask him to have you investigate. I'm not sure he will. Detective, I'm next. Or perhaps Okpara, then me. I can't say."

"Who else was there, when the bomb was found under your car?"

"My good friend and party member, Professor Nwikeki. He was accompanying me to the meeting. The meeting was cancelled after the bomb attempt, though, and changed to this Friday."

"Can I speak to him about this?"

"By all means. In fact, I insist."

I did not know whether to believe him or not. He studied me for a while. "You don't believe me. Do you?"

"I don't know quite what to believe."

"Fair enough. Speak to Sergeant Obiwali of the Metropolitan Police Division. He will corroborate all I have told you." He poured another drink, another small one.

I walked out of his house a lot less sure of myself than when I had walked in.

I drove over to the Metropolitan Police Division, which had jurisdiction of Rumuokoro. Sergeant Obiwali confirmed his information. He had taken the doctor's statement, showed it to me along with logs of the calls and a file on the bomb found under his car. If this was a lie, it came with backup. I was still suspicious—all this could be an elaborate charade to divert attention from the doctor. I needed someone not connected to him.

I drove to Professor Nwikeki's country home, not far away. He was a local politician, actively involved with the struggle for the Ogoni people, and he was chairman of the political Elders Forum. He was a good contact, someone I trusted. It only took him a few minutes to confirm what the doctor had told me. He thought Dr. Puene had nothing to do with either the Okpara bombing or the Wike murder. "I assure you Vincent is a good man. A very religious and respectable man."

"But couldn't it all be a hoax?"

"Not from what I know."

I left, drove back to headquarters slowly, trying to think it over.

Femi was not in our office when I got back. Before heading home, I decided to grab some food. I had eaten nothing since morning and I was almost famished.

I ran into Femi outside our building on my way to the *buka*.

He was looking downcast. I told him I could use some food. We walked into a nearby restaurant while I told him about my conversation with Dr. Puene. He said nothing. He just listened quietly. We took a table, me wondering what was up. He waited until I had ordered. "I have been reassigned."

I nodded. "It's nonsense." The waitress brought the first part of my order. I was hungrier than I'd realized. Femi watched me eat. I offered him some, but he shook his head.

"I've been meaning to ask you something," he said.

"About what?"

"Do you think we have a leak?" he asked.

How did he expect me to respond?

"Never occurred to me," I said, still regarding him closely, "Okay. What if there is one. Who could that be?"

He smiled grimly. "Hey. Nobody said anything about anybody being a leak." He adroitly avoided answering my question. He looked at me closely, then said, "Forget that I asked." He was on the edge but not yet ready to jump.

I finished, paid the waitress, and we left. As we walked back to headquarters and my car, he asked, finally, "Think you'll find out who's behind the killings?"

"I'm still convinced Puene's behind it all."

"So what are you going to do now?"

"I don't know. Why do you want to know?"

He just stared at me, then shook his head. "Sometimes you are so full of crap. We've known each other a long time. I'm just curious, that's all. Good luck with your sarcastic self, lieutenant."

I watched him walk back to headquarters and felt even more alone than before.

I got into my car, still watching Femi as he disappeared in the Yard. I sighed, picked up my cell phone, and called Freda.

"Hello, it's me," I said when she picked up.

"Yes, I gathered."

"I'm sorry about earlier on."

"It's okay. I'm sorrier," she said.

"You are."

"Funny."

"Someone is lovesick and not man enough to accept it."

She laughed.

"What are you doing right now?" I asked.

"I'm in the kitchen, preparing dinner."

"If it's okay, I'm going home, going to sleep, and not planning on getting up until tomorrow. Is that okay?"

"If that's what you want."

"I'm afraid I would not be good company."

"You're in my heart, Tammy."

For some reason, I did not know what to say except goodbye. I did not deserve her. And I had no idea what to do about it.

Or what to do about the murders.

I drove home and rested for a while, lying on my back on the bed. Sleep came quickly but it was restless.

CHAPTER SIXTEEN

The next morning around ten o'clock, as I parked, Okoro came out of our building, looking his usual unhappy self.

"Hi," he said. "We haven't seen Femi today. He didn't sign in this morning."

"Did you call his number?"

He nodded. "He switched off."

A few days ago I would have thought nothing of it. Now I started to worry about the worst. "Something could have happened to him," I told him.

His eyes widened in surprise. Instead of asking anything, he hurried away, putting distance between us.

I decided to check on Femi at home. I went back to my car, unlocked it, got inside. I drove over to his house and walked up to his front door. It was open.

Open. I did not like that.

I stepped inside. The apartment was dark. It was hot and smelled musty. I groped the wall until I felt the light switch and flipped it. The not-so-lavishly decorated apartment that the light revealed was just what one would expect from a police officer's salary. Not a rich man's paradise in a well-to-do neighborhood.

I almost made it through the living room before I saw the foot sticking out from underneath a padded settee. A man's foot. Wearing a dark sock and a fairly good quality black shoe. I did not need to guess whose foot it was.

I slowly walked around the settee and came face-to-face with Femi—or at least, face-to-face with what was left of his face. A bullet hole between his eyes definitely spoiled his boyish good looks. I did not bother taking his pulse, but instead bent down, lifted up his jacket, and pulled out his wallet, then went through the rest of his pockets. Nothing I found told me who had killed him or why.

I went back to my car and used the police radio to call in a formal report. A police officer was down: now everything had to be by the book—with a civilian you might cut corners, but not with one of your own. Then, with the sight of yet another dead body lingering in my mind, I stood against my car and lit a cigarette, even though I had no one to annoy with the smoke. A police officer down—that was disturbing, very disturbing.

Soon enough a police car drove up, followed by a van. Sergeant Okoro stepped out of the car and told me the pathologist would be arriving shortly. Officers from the van began to put up red tape and cordon off the area. There would always be onlookers. With few jobs, people had plenty of time.

I gave Okoro a cigarette and we blew smoke together while most of the forensics crew went into the apartment. I would just be in their way. Two of the forensics officers approached us, one with a camera, the other with a notepad.

"You know about this?" the one with the notepad asked me.

"I found the body, but that's all I know so far. No idea who did it, when, or why. He did not report for duty today, and I decided to check on him."

He nodded, then he and his partner went into the apartment to do their jobs. Okoro and I followed them, but stayed in the doorway. It was the usual busy crime scene. Officers collected evidence and placed it in bags. There was the periodic flash from a digital camera, recording elements of the scene. I saw three spent shells on the floor. There was a lot of blood on the carpet, but not much more than you would expect from a head shot. After a while, the pathologist showed up and began his inspection of the body before it was moved to the morgue.

"Can you get a clear shot of this?" Nnadozie asked the guy taking the pictures, pointing to a blood spatter on the wall. Another guy was carefully looking for any slugs that had gone through the dead man's head and out the other side. They were being thorough.

I remembered Femi's words from our last conversation.

I decided it was better not to tell Okoro about my conversation with Femi yesterday afternoon. He'd think I was losing it. Maybe I had already lost it, but if there was a leak as Femi implied, it could be anybody. Including Okoro.

After I left the scene, I drove to Freda's office. We went across the street to a small restaurant for drinks, and at a quiet table, I filled her in on everything. It felt important to tell her.

She did not want to accept it. Especially about Femi, that he had been murdered because of the Okpara case. "That's what my gut says," I told her. "But I have no proof, and with the restrictions Chief has placed on me, no way to get any. Not yet. I have to think. Let's get out of here." For once, she dropped work—she was as committed to her work as I was to mine. We got in my car and drove. I had no idea where I was driving to, and did not care.

"Tammy, I'm afraid," she finally said. "What are you going to do?"

"No idea."

It was too hot to think. I took us to another small restaurant and bar: the Grill Restaurant. The food was not very good, but the air conditioners made up for the menu. We both sat there, looking at the food we'd ordered, trying to digest Femi's death. Freda looked badly shaken. Me, I wished I could wake up and find this was all a bad dream. I gazed out the restaurant window without seeing.

"Tammy, how can you be certain Femi was murdered because of the case? Maybe he wasn't. Maybe it isn't as bad as that," Freda said, unable to stand the silence any longer. I looked up. She could see pain and weariness in my eyes.

"Hon," I said, "I'm praying you're right."

There was not much left to say. "What are you going to do now?"

"I've thought of one thing." I took out my cell and phoned Kola Badmus at *The Nigerian Chronicles*. I was in luck, he was in. He knew Femi was dead but didn't know the details. I told him that Femi had been shot—and then I really let it fly, telling him I thought Femi had been murdered because of the Okpara case and because of a leak within the force.

"Where do I meet you, Tammy?" Kola said immediately.

"I'm at the Grill Restaurant right now."

"I'll come over. Wait for me."

As I put away my cell phone, I knew Chief would not be happy with me. I did not care. Femi deserved the best.

"Mind telling me what *that* was about?" Freda asked. I could feel her pulling away from me, wondering about the phone call and what I was going to tell the reporter. I tried to change the subject. "So, darling. How are you holding up in the office?"

"Not bad. One very important client hasn't made up her mind to buy life insurance yet. Otherwise, it's all in order."

"Who is he?"

"*She.* The wife of the older brother of the Petroleum Minister."

"Professor Donald Chike?"

"You know him?"

"No, but I've certainly heard about him."

"I met her at a luncheon party. She seemed interested in our life insurance, so I've done one follow-up visit. She's almost hooked."

"It'll sure be a big account."

"I like the marketing part of my job the best. I like selling, finding where their interests and mine link up."

After that we ran out of conversation.

About twenty minutes later, a light green Mercedes 230 came to a standstill outside. Kola's tall, heavyset figure got out of the car and came into the restaurant. He was clutching a fat file.

I pulled out a chair and he sat with us. "This is Freda," I told him. "She's . . . a friend." She darted me a look as if to say, Why am I here? Good question. I had not thought this through—I had just jumped ahead.

He did not give her a second glance. "What's the story on the dead officer?" He took out a pad.

"I believe he found out some pretty hot shit, so he was killed."

I told him my conversation with Femi yesterday afternoon.

He was skeptical. I had expected that.

"I need facts, my friend."

"I don't have a lot of facts and I have no proof, but I suspect Femi was killed to prevent him from revealing any more than he already had."

"You want me to quote you directly." He said it flatly, not as a question. He knew what I was up to.

"It's one way to find out, isn't it? To get some hard evidence. If there's a leak, he'll think I'm a wild card. He'll come after me. Then I'll have my proof."

"You're being a fool." He thought it over. "I like it. It'll sell newspapers. Does Olatunji know about this?"

"No. He wouldn't let me if he knew."

He seemed pleased, but of course, Freda was the opposite: "My God, you've gone crazy. Is that what this is all about? Making yourself bait?"

My mind was already made up; it was made up by Femi's death. Perhaps it was crazy, but I owed him something. "They're going to come after me anyway. They know I won't give up. Life is too short to wait to be murdered."

Freda was shaking. "You could get killed, Tammy. Did you ever stop to think about that?" She glared at me. "And what about involving me? You've put me in the middle of this now."

"No one has to know about you," I replied hesitantly. I wanted to be angry with her, but she was right. Why had I brought her along, into danger? I turned back to Kola. "She's right. Let's leave her out of it. She wasn't here."

He nodded. He did not need her for the story anyway.

"About the rest of it, though. Are we on?"

"I have to talk to my editor. I'll call you in an hour."

After he left, I looked at Freda but she avoided my eyes. I could not blame her. We did not say a word during the drive to her office, and I could not blame her for that, either. She went inside without looking back. I could not blame her for anything.

I was on my own.

I did not want to go back to my office to stare at the walls, so I went to a small drinking pub a few blocks from headquarters. Police officers liked the place, and I felt like being among my own kind. I stepped inside and looked around. Instead of slapping me on the back, the other officers avoided my eyes. Great, just great.

I ordered whiskey and the bartender poured the drink. Then I looked around. And realized how self-absorbed I was. They were not ignoring me or shunning me. It was that I was not the only person affected by Femi's death. They were not just avoiding me, they were avoiding each other. We were all part of a family, and we were in mourning.

I downed the whiskey in one go. It burned all the way down. "Another," I told Benjamin, the bartender.

"I heard about your man," he said, pouring me another drink. "I'm sorry."

I nodded, not knowing what to say. I was drinking to get drunk. I was furious with Chief, with the entire police force, with the world, with everybody. I was on my third drink when my cell phone rang. I flipped it open, expecting Kola. It was Captain Akpan.

When I spoke my voice sounded dead. "Yes, captain?"

"Where are you, detective? Something came up."

"Something that has to do with me?"

"Where are you?"

"Near headquarters."

"In the bar?" His ears were sharp when it came to background sounds.

"I can come down to the office if you want."

"I just want to know if you know where a newspaper reporter—Kola Badmus—is. You were talking with him a few hours ago."

Just when I thought it could not get worse.

"His editor called, concerned. He was supposed to call in, but didn't. He's on what is considered a dangerous assignment and is supposed to check in regularly. If you were the last person to speak with him, do you have any idea what happened?"

"Wish I did," I said. I sat looking at the third drink in front of me. Suddenly, it did not feel like a good time to get drunk. "Shall I go down to the newspaper offices?"

"Good," was all Akpan told me.

CHAPTER SEVENTEEN

The Nigerian Chronicles had an office arrangement typical of a newspaper. Tunde Abiodun was the city editor. He was a fat, bald man with a fat, bald manner. He grimaced when he saw me walking up to him.

"Any word on Kola?" I asked him.

"I was hoping you would tell me."

"When did you see him last?"

"On his way to see you. He told me that you called him, that you had a story for him. He left to meet you. That was the last we heard of him. Did you meet him?"

"Yes. I gave him a story. He was going to come back here and talk with you about it."

"Then you should know more than me. What was the story?"

"I think Femi, my assistant, found out something too hot and he was murdered. I was willing to put my name on the story."

He nodded. "Well, he never made it back here. And I think I have the right to hold you at least partially responsible."

There was nothing I could say except that I would do my best to find Kola. He did not seem to think my best meant very much. Then I went up one flight of stairs to see Sheun Daramola, the owner. He outranked the city editor. I had never met him, but he had a reputation even tougher than Abiodun's.

"Homicide?" he asked. He removed his glasses. What was with these old guys removing their glasses when they wanted to talk? "Sit down."

I sat.

"Do you have any news about my reporter?"

"Nothing yet. I'd like to look through his office, to see if there's anything there that might be useful."

He nodded. "Anything that would help. We are running stories in today's paper, and the other papers are donating space to run stories as well. In something like this, we stick together."

"I may have to talk to his colleagues."

"No problem. I'll have you shown to his office. I had it locked up when it was obvious there was something wrong." He called on the phone for the city editor, and when the fat man came in, panting from the effort of walking, Daramola told him to show me to Kola's office. "I don't know how going through Kola's things will help, but do whatever the detective asks. If he wants to speak with other reporters, arrange it."

The city editor nodded and led me out. We went back downstairs, past several offices to a locked one. Abiodun produced a bunch of keys from his pocket and unlocked the door, then excused himself and returned to his own desk.

The office was something of a mess, but it was a working mess, with file folders covering the desk and most of the floor. My guess was each folder had its own specific place. I started with the desk. The papers yielded nothing. I found a daybook, which looked like his backup. His appointments were all listed. He'd met a council chairman an hour before seeing me. I opened each drawer of his desk, but in the end, it was a waste. The files on the floor provided nothing, either. I went to talk with the staff, but none of them knew anything, including other stories Kola had been covering; competition for stories could be fierce, and Kola was usually tight-lipped about his work right until it appeared on the front page. Soon enough I was driving back to headquarters with nothing to show for my visit.

While driving, I phoned Akpan on my cell. "Any luck finding Kola?"

"No. We've checked the hospitals and morgues. Nothing."

"No body but also no sign of kidnapping? No ransom demand?"

"No."

Back in my office, I found a new assistant detective, already hard at work writing reports. Writing reports about what, I did not know. I felt uneasy, seeing him in Femi's seat. Perhaps Chief was feeling guilty, and was giving me back a partner. The new man said that he was just graduated from the Police Detective College. This was his first field experience. His name was Ade, and he was also from Yoruba, like Chief. Was Ade there to work for me or to spy on me?

After he introduced himself, he told me that Chief had Femi's file, and wanted to see me. I spent a few minutes getting to know him, then went up to Chief's office. Stella waved me in and went back to her Imperial. I wondered why she kept the typewriter. She also had a computer. Perhaps it was easier to keep certain documents confidential if there was only a single typed copy.

Chief's door was half open. I pushed and entered.

"You wanted to see me?" I asked a little stiffly, wary.

"Yes, Tammy. At ease. Kola Badmus. You were the last person to see him?" He closed the file he had been reading, removed his glasses, laid them carefully on the desk in front of him.

"Yes. Kola is a friend."

"What were you talking with him about?"

"Stuff. We hadn't had a drink together for some time, so I asked him to join Freda and me at the Grill. We had a few drinks and he left."

He pressed a button on the intercom. "Have Captain Akpan bring Miss Agboke in."

The door opened and Freda entered, Captain Akpan behind her.

"Honey?" Freda asked me as soon as she saw me. "What's this all about?"

"Sit down, Miss Agboke," Chief told her. She sat. "Miss Agboke, you and my detective had drinks with Kola Badmus today. Is that correct?"

"Yes." She looked from him to me, then back to him.

"What did the three of you talk about?"

"Nothing much. We know Kola Badmus and we've become friends. You know. Chitchat. Why is it important? Why was I brought here?"

"Because the reporter has disappeared. Because a major investigation has already been disrupted and may now have been compromised altogether."

Freda looked at me. "I don't know anything about that."

"Was Kola taking notes?"

"He said something about a story idea."

"About what?"

"He didn't say. I mentioned some things my company has been up to. I suggested a story about marketing. He liked that idea and wrote down something about it." Freda was on top of it now. She had gone from nervous to calm and very believable, not missing a beat.

Chief looked at her, then smiled his polite official smile. "Very well. My apologies for bringing you down here. But you can appreciate why."

"No, I can't."

His smile hardened. "You may now go. Captain, please see to it that she gets back safely to her home."

"I can see myself back safely, thank you," she said coolly. "I'd like to have a word with Tammy."

"Not right now. I have some more questions for him. A journalist is missing, remember. You can speak to him after he's done. Good day." He simply dismissed her. But Freda was not the type of person you dismissed, simply or otherwise.

"Fine. But I do not appreciate being harassed. Next time you want me to come down here, talk to my lawyer first. And I'll be speaking with my CEO about this." Chief said nothing—her CEO was Mr. Daniel Chukwu, CEO of Mercury Insurance and a very powerful and respected man. She stood, looked once at me—not very happy with me, either—and walked out briskly, followed by Captain Akpan.

Chief looked at the empty doorway for a while, then at me. "You, too. Go. You're dismissed."

I said nothing to Stella on my way out, nor did she say anything to me.

I managed to get out of headquarters in time to see Akpan and Freda walking to his car. "Hey. Captain, I'll take her," I told Akpan.

He looked at me as seriously as he ever had. "Chief is through with you?"

"For now. Want to tell me what's going on?"

"From what he says, you should be telling us."

Well, that nailed it. At least Akpan was direct with me.

Freda came over to me and we went to my car, leaving Akpan behind, watching. And he obviously was not the only one watching.

I drove her back to her apartment. Neither of us said much. As soon as we got to her place, Freda left me in the living room and went to have a cold bath, to wash the heat away. I admired her style and status. She had pushed back at Chief by mentioning her CEO.

I sat and flipped through a magazine, not reading, while Freda had her bath and changed her clothes. She then prepared us a dinner of *jollof* rice cooked with fried frozen fish.

"Smells good," I said as we sat down to eat.

"Mom's quite the cook," Freda said. "I inherited her culinary skills. If you like this, I cook *Odikaikon* soup even better."

"Sounds good!"

The chatter was not much, and died down as we ate. There was too much for us to think about. We did not talk about Kola. She had never met him before today. In my stolen glances I could see she was worried, worried about me. Finally, she said, "Am I crazy, or is your chief of police acting as if he is investigating you?"

"It is starting to feel like it, but no. No, honey. I don't think that's it."

"This is getting out of hand. You're going to get hurt."

I nodded. She was right, but that changed nothing. "I'm sorry I got you involved. I never should have met Kola with you there. I wasn't thinking."

"No, you weren't."

"But I'm thinking now. And I think the less I involve you, the better."

"It's a little late for that." She was not about to let me push her away.

She was holding up fairly well, but I told her she shouldn't stay here. I could tell she didn't want to go. Freda, although open to the idea of going away to someplace safe, did not want to leave me.

"Coffee?" she asked. I nodded, and she went into the kitchen and poured two cups from an already prepared pot and returned to hand me a cup. It was good.

"I feel safer with you," she answered, sipping from her cup.

I shook my head, drank more coffee. "Freda, it's dangerous around me. How about if I take you to your aunts' for a few days?"

She nodded her acceptance.

My cell phone began to ring. I pulled it from my pants pocket.

"Ignore it," she said. It was not a request.

I looked at the caller ID. "It's Captain Akpan," I said. "He'd never call this late unless it was important." I turned away from her and flipped open the cell. "Yes, captain?"

"Kola Badmus, the newspaper guy. We've found him. Dead. In his car, in the trunk. On the East-West Road." He gave me a cross street.

"When was he found?"

"About half an hour ago."

"Someone will have to call his wife."

"I'm looking after that."

"Thank you, captain." I flipped the phone closed.

"The reporter?" she asked.

"Yes. They found him. Probably I got him killed, just talking to me," I said to her. "I have to do something. I owe him."

She knew she could not stop me so she let me go. Outside, I looked up at a dark sky of shimmering stars millions of miles from Earth. "God," I muttered, "what is the point?" I got no answer—not today, anyway.

I drove toward East-West Road. It was way out of my district. When I got there, the site was crawling with blue uniforms setting up floodlights. It looked like a battlefield, with Captain Akpan as the general issuing orders. Except the fighting was already over.

I saw Ade, my new partner, before he saw me. "Fill me in," I asked him.

"Officers Ubani and Dan found the car. They were smart enough to check the car's engine—it was still hot. They found Kola in the trunk, shot several times. Looks like handguns. He was tied up. They radioed it in. An alert was put out for any suspicious-looking persons in the area. Maybe we'll get very lucky."

I shook my head. "I doubt it. They planned this well. They probably left no dangling loose ends."

"Captain thinks that whoever dropped off the car might still be in the area, so we're searching it. Captain does not think they thought we would find the car so soon."

"He's certainly right about them maybe being in the area, given the engine was still hot. There are no tire tracks, but I see some footprints. Looks like perhaps two people drove him here, then left him. Okporo Road is walking distance from here. They could lose themselves in the area quickly, and could vanish more easily on foot than in a car. But perhaps they had an escape car waiting for them on that paved road over there, where no tracks would be left. Let's hope Forensics can tell us something."

Ade tried to keep his eyes from growing wider as I rambled on about the different possibilities. I let him be. He was inexperienced—by definition all my former partners had also been inexperienced when they first started. So had I, or any other police officer.

I walked over to view the body. The trunk lid was open. Ade was behind me. I hoped he had the stomach for this. Kola's face was bruised, bloodied at his nose and mouth. They had been hard on him before shooting him. It looked as if he had been shot and then dumped in the trunk.

Ade said, quietly, "He was shot three times in the head. The pathologist said the first bullet probably killed him instantly." I could see that. Ade was talking to ease his tension. He was breathing hard, almost panting. He wanted to look away from the corpse but did not want to lose face with his new partner. Maybe it was better to lose face than to lose dinner.

Nnadozie was trying to lift fingerprints from the car. One of his boys found a pistol in the dirt a few feet away.

Captain Akpan walked over. "You just got here?"

"Just a few minutes ago," I said.

One of Nnadozie's crew came over. The pistol they'd found, which was likely the murder weapon, was a .22. Four shells were missing from the clip. It had been fired recently. Probably used elsewhere, then dumped here. Tape around the handle—I'd seen this before—to prevent the lifting of fingerprints. Professionals.

Dr. Onwuchekwa cleared Kola's corpse for the trip to the morgue, and there was nothing more to do except wait for lab results. I couldn't see going back to Freda's, to wake her up to hear about more horrors. I decided to go home and get some rest. I told Ade to do the same, and to prepare a report first thing tomorrow. When I told Akpan I was heading home, he just looked at me and nodded. "The autopsy's tomorrow morning at 8:30. Be there."

I nodded. "Of course, captain. Good night."

"Good night," he repeated.

When I returned to my apartment, I removed my clothes and slipped on a pair of boxer shorts and an undershirt. I turned my cell off, then turned off the ringer on the home phone so nothing would wake me up. For the moment, everything could wait. I set the alarm for 7:00 A.M., made sure all the doors and windows were locked, slipped a wooden chair under the kitchen doorknob so no one could open it without making a lot of noise. Then I did the same for the front door. I laid my piece down beside me, closed my eyes, and it all went dark.

CHAPTER EIGHTEEN

A buzzing woke me up. I groaned, shut off the alarm, went back to sleep. But after maybe half an hour I woke again, this time for good. Rubbing my face helped wake me up—it hurt. I put the phones back on. When I checked my cell, there were two messages. The first was Freda. She wanted to see how I was doing, and was not happy I had switched off my cell. The second message was also from her, but this time she wanted me to call her. I was not sure I wanted to talk to anyone just yet—but I dialed anyway.

"Why did you switch off your phone?" she asked immediately, anxiety in her voice.

"I needed to have some sleep, that's all."

"You could have called when you got back to your place."

I knew she was frightened and needed some reassurance. "It was late by the time I was done. It was a murder scene. If I'd called,

I would have woken you up. I was going to call you this morning. Where are you? In your office?"

"I'm at home," she said curtly.

"You didn't go to work today?"

"I called in sick. I'm frightened. I can't reach you, you turn off your phones—what did you expect me to do? I barely feel safe hiding in my apartment."

"I'll come over as soon as I can, okay?"

"That's better."

I knocked on her door exactly twenty-three minutes later. "Good morning, honey," I said.

"Thank God you're here!" She had already packed a bag.

She locked the door behind her.

As we drove to her aunts' house, we talked about how hot it was. When we got there, she took her suitcase, kissed me, and went inside. I could see her through the windows saying hello to her aunts. She did not come back out. I drove off and headed toward the city morgue, wondering how this day would go, wondering whether I would live through it, wondering whether I would ever see Freda again.

Port Harcourt was very active at this time of day. Workers on their way to their jobs had jammed the traffic by the time I got to Eastern Bypass.

My route took me straight to the General Hospital—Port Harcourt's morgue. Captain Akpan and Sergeant Okoro were already there, along with the pathologist and his assistant. The autopsy was just beginning. It did not take very long—this pathologist was quick. Captain Akpan informed me that the .22 found at the scene was the weapon used to kill Kola.

"The victim was tortured," he said, showing me cigarette burns on the corpse's chest. "Whoever did this has watched too many mafia films. It probably went on two, maybe three, hours before he was shot and killed."

I told Captain Akpan that Thompson was the likely killer of Kola. I was almost certain ballistics would prove the same gun shot Wike, after all.

Once the autopsy was done, I drove back to my apartment—it checked out okay. For a while, I sat around, just thinking. I did not want to call Freda or anyone else. But I could not stay alone in my apartment.

I left abruptly and, on a whim, drove down to the Protea Hotel. I needed to get away to think. The Protea Hotel was cool and exclusive, a perfect place to think. And I was hungry. At the very least, I'd get an excellent meal.

I took a seat and immediately a waiter came over. I decided on fried rice with salad and chicken, and some choice red wine.

As I sipped the wine, I looked up to see Okpara walk into the lobby with a younger man. I had seen the younger man somewhere but could not immediately place him. Nice suit, nice hands. The hands seemed familiar. Calluses. And then I remembered. The younger man was the fellow I had seen on Tuesday in Chief's office.

Well, how about that?

I watched them walk to the elevators and go into one. From where I sat, I could see that the elevator stopped on the sixth floor.

Minutes later, Chief walked into the lobby. No uniform today. He wore jeans and a T-shirt with a fez cap. The outfit was odd for him, and he looked awkward. If you did not know who he was, you would not think he was a senior officer. But it was Chief, all right.

I watched him walk directly to the elevators, and take one to the sixth floor.

Well, how about that?

I sat there for a short while, letting it sink in. That floor was getting crowded. But what I saw next was a slap in the face.

A moment later, Barigha Duncan, supposed boss of the Duncan gang, walked into the lobby. What timing. He also took an elevator. It stopped on the sixth floor.

Well, how about that, indeed?

My mentor was involved with Okpara. And Barigha. Police, politicians, and criminals—meeting privately in a hotel room.

I drank the rest of the wine.

When I walked into the lobby, I looked for and saw what I had hoped: surveillance cameras. Which would provide proof. Proof at least that they were all in the same hotel at the same time. The cameras also seemed to cover the elevators—proof they all went to the same floor.

I approached the hotel manager, showed him my badge, and asked him about the security system, in particular the cameras. There were cameras throughout the hotel. We went into the security office. Soon enough I had confiscated the lobby videotape along with the tapes recorded just now on the sixth floor.

A friend of mine, Phil, runs Global Video at Rumuola. He would be helpful. As I drove to his place, I regularly checked my rearview mirror.

I called Phil on my cell.

"Good afternoon," his thick voice answered.

"Phil, it's Tammy."

"Tammy? Long while, buddy."

"It's dark-clouds time. I need you."

"Name it."

"I have some security tapes. I need to watch them, transfer them to digital, and make a few copies."

"Is this police work?"

"Yes. But it's even worse than that. You don't want to know."

"Well, come on by then, I'll be here. You piqued my interest."

"I'm already on my way. See you in ten."

It did not take that long to reach his shop. I parked my car behind the building and went in through the back door. If I was being followed, there was no point making it easy for them to find me.

Phil was a thin man whose face barely seemed to have room for his wide grin.

"Okay," he said. "Hand them over."

"Can I do this myself? Without involving you?"

"No."

"It would be healthier for you, my friend."

He looked at me steadily, his grin gone. "You would not know where to begin."

I sighed. "Okay. But I was never here."

The grin did not return.

We sat at a console and he loaded the lobby tape. It was not hard to find the shots of Chief and his "friends" entering the lobby and then going into elevators. The security cameras on the sixth floor were particularly significant—we saw each of them enter the same hotel room. Watching my mentor go into that hotel room made me sick. I wanted to close my eyes, to shut the damn machine off, to wipe the memory of the tapes clean. But you cannot stop watching a rushing train become a wreck.

I watched Phil push some buttons and make a digital version of the important sections of the two tapes, then burn some CDs. With his equipment and expertise, it did not take long. When he was finished, he handed me several CDs and a Zip drive, each containing the digital versions of the tapes.

As I left, I saw him checking for the pistol he kept under the counter.

I planned my next move. It was not enough to have Chief on tape, meeting with Barigha and Okpara. I must have proof of his relationship with those two, plus the identity and role of Mr. Calluses. I drove to my bank, got access to my safety deposit box, and put one of the CDs into it. That was my safety net. Then, back in my car, I flipped open my cell phone and dialed Chief's direct cell line. I had no idea what I would say specifically, but I knew the generalities.

"Hello?"

"It's Tammy, Chief."

"Tammy. What do you want?"

"I have a tape showing you, Okpara, and the young man I ran into leaving your office a few days ago. All meeting together. Made me sick to watch you and your pals, Chief."

"What pals? What are you talking about?" His "surprise" was not convincing.

"You, Okpara, the friend of yours I saw in your office days ago—and Barigha Duncan. You all met at the Protea Hotel today. The room number was 666. Appropriate, isn't it?"

"I don't know what you're talking about."

"Sure you do, Chief. I was there. I saw you. And I saw you again on the hotel security tapes."

Silence.

I visualized him thinking, quickly sorting through his options. "Don't do anything stupid," he finally said. "Bring the recordings to me. We will work something out."

"Chief, you know better."

"Wise up. You don't know what you are up against. Bring

the evidence to me. I will make it all go away, just as if nothing happened."

"There are a lot of people dead, including a police officer. I'm coming to see you to settle it all." I hung up before I could say anything else. Things kept getting worse, but they could not get that much worse. We were near the end. My hope was Chief would pull a terrific rabbit from his hat.

CHAPTER NINETEEN

It was not long, on my way to headquarters, before the white Toyota truck appeared in my rearview mirror. I sped up; so did it. I saw Thompson in the passenger seat, Mr. Gorilla driving. Eastern Bypass is always deserted. The first shot shattered the passenger window behind me. They were not about to leave me alive this time. I floored the gas but the Toyota swerved into me, forcing me off the road. My car found a tree. My head and the steering wheel made friends.

The Toyota drove off the road toward me. Thompson and Mr. Gorilla emerged, each carrying an equally nasty-looking pistol. I shook my head, getting my brains back together as Thompson walked to the driver's side window while Mr. Gorilla stood pointing his gun at me.

Some blood trickled down my face, but not into my eyes.

Thompson yanked the door open, grabbed me by the collar,

and roughly dragged me out of my car. I punched him in the gut and he doubled over in pain. Mr. Gorilla stopped me by shoving his pistol between my eyes. "Don't do that again," he snarled. Then he pushed me against the car and took my pistol from its holster. He looked inside my car. The glove compartment had popped open and the surveillance CDs had spilled out. He opened the door and grabbed them. Now they had them all—except for the one in my safety deposit box.

Thompson was gasping for breath, holding his stomach. He slowly stood, cursed me, and punched me in the stomach, to return the favor.

A cell phone rang, with a *Star Wars* theme. It was Thompson's. He flipped it open. "Yes, sir. We have him and the recordings." He gave the caller our location. Then we all waited. Me and the two guys who wanted to kill me.

I think the wait was harder on them.

After maybe twenty minutes, a black Ford Expedition rolled up. The same one Howell Osamu had stepped into. The driver stepped out. He held an Uzi. Getting out of the backseat was Barigha Duncan. He looked at me as I stood holding my stomach, leaning against the car, waiting. His two thugs stood on either side of me.

He must have seen the look on my face when I saw him step out of the SUV.

"You never reckoned to have to deal with me. You see, you were interfering with my plans. I set Okpara up to run for the statehouse. And you see, he must win."

It felt like another blow to my stomach hearing Barigha speak. So Okpara was part of the Duncan gang. Barigha had even more sinister plans. If and when he succeeded, he would become untouchable. It certainly explained the killings.

"I suppose Olatunji called you?"

Barigha lit a cigar instead. The smoke he blew in my face was expensive. I acted as if I was still dazed. They all bought it.

"The CDs," he demanded, still staring into my face but asking one of his men. Thompson handed him the disks. "Where are the original tapes?" Barigha demanded. He looked at me. "Never mind. We will find them eventually." He looked around. It was quiet. No witnesses.

A cell phone rang, but no *Star Wars* theme this time. Barigha pulled a cell from his pocket. "Okpara. Hello." He listened. "Yes, I am on my way. Something came up, but nothing I can't handle. Don't get yourself worked up. No. Okay. Bye."

I looked at Barigha. "So Dr. Puene was telling the truth all along, and Okpara was lying. Thompson here was never working for Dr. Puene. He's working for you. And Okpara. What will happen now?" I asked him.

"Unlike some, I have no problem with your being dead. In fact, by now I am rather looking forward to it. You will be found dead in your car, I think. A tragic accident." He sounded like a judge reading my sentence. "You should have driven more carefully," he said, and then laughed to himself.

"Why kill Femi?" I asked.

"You have your Chief of Police to thank for that."

"Chief would not do that."

"Sure he did. Femi saw Olatunji with me. So he was a threat to the whole plan."

"So who tried to blow up Okpara?"

"My, you want to know a lot, don't you. Is this a bad movie, where everything is summed up at the end? Okay, fine. Somehow Puene had discovered the bomb under his car. Angus was preparing another bomb meant for Puene's house and it detonated prematurely, injuring him. But it all worked well for a diversion."

"And all the other dead?"

He shrugged.

"What about Wike, Okpara's personal assistant? What threat did he make?"

"His mistake was calling Okpara to say that he had spotted your car around his home. He couldn't keep his cool. Okpara called me to say that Wike needed to be taken care of or he'd give our plan away. Wike was a smart man but he was soft." He looked at Thompson and smiled. "Thompson, here, on the other hand, is a great kid. I'm proud of him. If he keeps up the good work, he'll head to the top. But enough. I don't have to tell you anything more, detective, except good-bye. I've had enough of you being protected."

I was glad I had hidden a digital recorder on me. Now all I had to do was stay alive.

"Thompson, he's all yours," Barigha said. The driver passed his Uzi to Thompson, then he and Barigha turned to leave.

"So long, Tammy," Barigha said.

"I have other copies. And you still don't have the original."

"Nice try."

"Embarrassing for you when someone else sees it."

"No one else will see it. And if they do, they'll know who their friends should be."

They all chuckled, and while they were expecting nothing from me, I hit Thompson in the jaw. As he fell back, I grabbed the Uzi.

Once I had the Uzi, it was not so tough. Nothing is that tough if you have an Uzi.

Mr. Gorilla and the driver reached for their pistols but the quick bursts from the Uzi were faster. They fell, as did Thompson. It was not hard. All I had to do was pull back on the trigger. Suddenly they were dead. Suddenly it was just Barigha Duncan and me. He reached into his jacket for his own gun but stopped as I leveled the Uzi at him. I could have shot him. I almost did. Instead, I gave him firsthand knowledge of what it felt like to be punched in the stomach.

He writhed on the ground for a while, surrounded by ex-employees who had recently suffered an abrupt termination. I took the CDs and threw them into the Explorer. Then, getting a pair of cuffs from my car, I hooked him up to the steering wheel of my damaged car. I took away his cell phone.

"Where are you going? You can't leave me here like this," he shouted at me.

"Sure I can. I'm borrowing your SUV. I have an appointment with Chief Olatunji. Don't worry. I'll tell someone you're here."

I got into his car and drove off, leaving him surrounded by death.

I made one call on the way. When I arrived, Stella was not there. Chief's front office was deserted, but his door was open. From inside I heard him say, in that deep voice, "Come in, Tammy. I've been expecting you."

I thought I heard a tinge of pride in his voice, pride that I had turned up alive. He had taught me well.

I walked into his office. He sat behind his desk, his hands folded over his stomach, looking at me.

We just stared at each other for a while. There was no need for talking.

Finally, I said, "I have the evidence, sir. The tapes showing you, Barigha, Okpara, and your young friend. I never got his name."

"George Minima."

"Who is he anyway?"

"Okpara's campaign manager."

"Hmm. I guess he's probably going to jail with the rest of you."

"You think so?" His eyes were unwavering. So were mine. "How does one million naira sound?" he asked.

"I don't care about the easy life, Chief. You disappoint me. What do you think your antigang crew would think? And please don't tell me that meeting with those criminals was part of your police work. No one would believe that."

"Everyone cares about the easy life."

I thought more. "Maybe. Okay, how does three million sound instead?"

"Two."

"How about two and a half?"

He blinked, then frowned, realizing he could not buy me.

"You wanted me dead, Chief."

"You have it all wrong. I never wanted you dead. That is why you are still alive. Port Harcourt depends on pretending, Tammy. I do a lot of good as chief of police. I turn my eye to the rest. Someone has to balance the interests of the citizens against organized crime and the oil companies. Tammy, I kept order in Port Harcourt."

"What a crusader you are. What about Femi?"

"I was sorry about Femi, but I was left with only one choice. I have not personally killed anyone for a long time. I've been able to leave that to others." He sighed, and finally looked away from me. "It won't work with you, will it?"

"No."

I opened my suit jacket, to show him the mike and tape recorder. "We're done," I said loudly, over my shoulder. Behind me, I heard Captain Akpan and his men walk in from the hallway, where they had been waiting.

"It's over, Chief."

"Is this what I taught you?"

"Yes."

"I was like your father."

"You were grooming me. Eventually you would have wanted me to kill for you."

"I was grooming you, Tammy, yes. But you killing anyone was never part of the plan." He smiled with no humor, and in his eyes, for the first time, I saw a deeper hurt than I had ever seen in anyone before. "I had other people for that."